A CLEAR CALLING

A CLEAR CALLING

DAVID AUSTIN

Jonathan Cape
London

Published by Jonathan Cape 2004

2 4 6 8 10 9 7 5 3 1

Copyright © David Austin 2004

David Austin has asserted his right under the Copyright, Designs
and Patents Act 1988 to be identified as the author of this work

First published in Great Britain in 2004 by
Jonathan Cape
Random House, 20 Vauxhall Bridge Road, London SW1V 2SA

Random House Australia (Pty) Limited
20 Alfred Street, Milsons Point, Sydney,
New South Wales 2061, Australia

Random House New Zealand Limited
18 Poland Road, Glenfield,
Auckland 10, New Zealand

Random House South Africa (Pty) Limited
Endulini, 5A Jubilee Road, Parktown 2193, South Africa

The Random House Group Limited Reg. No. 954009
www.randomhouse.co.uk

A CIP catalogue record for this book is available from the British Library

ISBN 0-224-06441-X

Papers used by Random House are natural,
recyclable products made from wood grown in sustainable forests;
the manufacturing processes conform to the environmental
regulations of the country of origin

Typeset by Palimpsest Book Production Limited
Polmont, Stirlingshire
Printed and bound in Great Britain by
Mackays of Chatham PLC

For Ma and Pop

My affectionate thanks to Doris Lessing for her
enduring support and encouragement.

A CLEAR CALLING

ONE

O^{N A FERRY} crossing a river, a boy of around twelve, his face turned downwards, broods over the churning water. He is tall, rangy, with a pretty, girlish face set under cropped blond hair. He balances his weight on one leg, while his other is crossed in front of him and propped up on the tip of his highly polished shoe. Altogether it might appear elegant, almost balletic, if he were not wearing the full uniform – considerably too big for him – of a naval officer, or rather, a naval officer cadet. The boy's body moves as though hindered by the stiff, unfamiliar uniform. It is this inconsonance between uniform and manner which magnifies his awkwardness – and his age. Around him, and at the rail, more passengers appear, gazing absently through the milky sunlight.

There is a moment when the boy appears so mesmerised by the swirl of water that there seems a danger he might allow himself to be drawn into it. But by the time the ferry is in mid-stream he is staring towards the receding bank, which now stretches wider before him. He searches, without moving his eyes, for some place, some thing, left behind.

At a point in his very young life when he'd first seen sailors' uniforms, he'd fallen in love with the idea of becoming a sailor himself. Of course, it was only the idea. Perhaps it would have been altogether better if he'd been given one of those sailor suits the Victorians were so fond of. Perhaps then his ambition might not have endured like much that is prohibited. And perhaps the conviction that he was possessed of a strong calling would not have eventually germinated in the minds of his parents. In its turn, their belief naturally reinforced his own; from his earliest recollections, he had fantasised about running away to sea. In his mind, it had become his destiny, a consolation increasingly, an excuse to himself, for anything he did not want to do, or failed at. In large part, it became who he was. Perhaps it was all there was.

The dream never properly left him: it was always there in some measure, and eventually interfered so much with his school work that his teachers thought him backward. In the end it became his solace, his comfort. It was with him wherever he went, whatever he did, growing stronger. He was somehow preserved, protected by it, as though behind it, despite his growing older, his body getting bigger, his face maturing, his voice breaking, some part of him remained anchored for ever in his young childhood. And so, as in some grand solution, it was thought best by his pecunious parents to send him to a nautical school. It seemed the obvious thing. And as far as he was concerned, it would not be stretching it to say he was overjoyed at the prospect. After all, now he could begin properly to create the image of a young seafarer. And in due course, that is exactly what he set about doing. He affected a kind of seamanlike walk, with a roll of the shoulders. He believed that, always searching the brilliant horizon, sailors must squint through narrowed eyes, and he began to do just that, as he imagined the articulations of the tropic sun and wind and reflections of the sea itself about his own face. He was possessed of a powerful imagination and his image of himself so perfectly matched his uniform there was hardly a gap to show. To some people it might have seemed comical, but to his nautical instructors, who had known little beyond their own seafaring, it was no more than living testimony to a boy's true calling.

There were times though, at the beginning, when this veneer – convincing as it was – was penetrated, revealing the child. The rules at this establishment were so many, so varied, so confusing, that for a time at least, it seemed as if he were permanently avoiding ambush. But he had no argument with the status quo; after all, it supported his dream which had become his life, though occasionally it could not be helped that he found himself outside its laws. It was at these times that the image he had cultivated could momentarily disappear, when – as was common in this kind of establishment – a silent, frightened child was hauled across a gym horse to be caned. Of course, for him, there was no real telling to what extent he had disengaged himself from the real world, only that in the process he had taken in everyone, including himself. But in time, the highly organised life at the nautical school did become his armour. He followed it comprehensively, and more or less unthinkingly. Its labyrinthine traditions and codes, in some strange way, maintained and preserved within him the young child, the imagined incunabula of a seafarer. He grumbled of course, along with his friends, about the lack of freedom, the food, the pettiness, but this was merely conformity of another kind. He understood, though he dared not admit it, that he liked to conform, liked being told where to be, at what time, what to do, how to do it, and liked to complain about it. Thinking, reflection, was not required. He was a particle flowing with all the other particles around an elaborate daily circuit, which, once learnt, required little thought. There was no need to question. What's more, in the daily congregational singing and wailing of psalms, he found himself rewarded with a deepening security. He began to develop a faith as well as a dream, and the sailor in his head with its dreamt adversities, became a Godfearing one.

TWO

THE LITTLE SPLASH of publicity which Robert Radnor had attracted on his return from India had sustained his identity for the rest of his days. He had lived in the warmth of its flame ever since. He'd done no work, no work that is in the conventional sense. He'd kept himself occupied, tended his vegetable garden, built boats from driftwood, and there'd been the wood carving, but no paid work. He'd felt neither the need nor the inclination.

The small amount of money he'd saved whilst at sea, added to the proceeds from the book, had allowed him some freedom, just a little independence, with which he'd gorged himself. Any ambition he may have had had been dissipated during a long and painful war. He'd been sunk, taken prisoner, redeemed, and suffered it all a second time, and the effect seems to have been to stop him talking. Or, you might say, to stop him altogether.

The people who lived locally, with one or two exceptions, notably Mrs Morrow the postmistress, were pleased to have an old eccentric living, not amongst them, but nearby, at a sober distance. It may be that through their preoccupation with appearance (they were mostly young and well-heeled) they were intrigued by him. They tolerated his sullen rudeness, even courted it for fun as children do, because they saw him as interesting, adding colour to the neighbourhood, even giving a Sunday afternoon walk with friends down from London a purpose, a glimpse, if they were lucky, of this comically unsociable old man, who at one time or another was supposed to have been something of a hero.

He lived, and had done since his return, a little over a mile from the ancient fishing village of Hevingbroke, which had now become, like so many such places, a smart residential reserve competing with itself. In contrast, it was a rough mile to Radnor's place and, in winter, muddy, down a deeply rutted farm track which tunnelled through tangled woodland leading at last to the little frontiersman's shack where he lived only a few yards above the shore on the River Orwell.

People who went there were certain to understand that they were not welcome. He would not speak to make his feelings understood. If he saw anyone too close, he would often jeer and spit in an uncontrollable, preposterous rage. And there were 'Keep Out' notices splashed in paint and nailed to the tumbledown field gate which he kept chained and padlocked, and bound with barbed wire. In the summer, sitting on a log on the beach or sprawled out on the shingle, he would wave people away and roar at them in a frightening, hilarious manner, cursing them to hell for their infernal snooping.

His hatred of everybody, and what he saw as the waste and emptiness of modern life, together with his own inability to find some meaning, kept his village trips to a minimum. He made the journey once or twice a month, less if he could manage; a burly man in his nineties and still well over six feet, his long white hair and beard blowing out sideways in the wind as he lumbered past the smartly refurbished, colour-washed cottages and brightly polished cars, hands

6

clasped behind his back, his mouth working unceasingly, in silent denigration.

His arrivals at the post office stores were moments of regret for Mrs Morrow. He was incapable, it seemed to her, of a civil word; or any word, for that matter. Incapable certainly of answering or commenting on her many fatuous and unhelpful remarks on the weather or the latest news, something in which he had not the slightest interest. It didn't help matters either when she fussed around him, driven more by an innate wariness than any real desire to help, advancing and retreating like a frightened, irresolute dog, anxious that his visit should pass without incident. She shrank back when he moved too close, rushing forward again when the danger had passed, following him all around the little store. It was a kind of dance which, in its way, symbolised her own ambivalence. Once, he became so irritated by all this that he swatted her away, narrowly missing her with a huge hand.

It always happened that between his visits, just as she was beginning to forget about him again, Radnor would re-appear to threaten her certainty, or uncertainty. The trouble was, he had spent so long on his own that even had he wished to, he'd lost any confidence in his ability to converse, almost lost the use of speech altogether. Sometimes he appeared timid and diffident in company and yet so unaware that he might fart or belch without the slightest recognition. When he had gone, taking with him an old canvas kitbag full of groceries which he hoisted on to his back, she would scuttle about squirting air spray in huge vaporous question marks around the shop, before standing at the door in silent confusion, her hands on her hips, watching him trudge away, bent low under his burden, towards the trees and the plains of mud, marvelling at such prodigious strength and independence in one so old.

Perhaps it was the thought that he threatened the

respectability of the neighbourhood which she found most vexing. It had been something from which she herself had derived a great deal of comfort in the past, this respectability. Though she had to admit that these days she was beginning not to like that sort of admission much. After all, she'd begun to argue with herself, he did no one any actual harm living down there in that shabby little hut. For the most part he kept out of everyone's way. If anything, it was they who sought him out. The fact that in the warmer weather he'd work on his boats or in his little vegetable patch without a stitch on was neither here nor there, really. Why shouldn't he? And if no one had gone spying on him, no one would have known about it. The thing was, living on his own for so long, he'd probably forgotten much of the common manner that went on between people. Deep within herself, she supposed, she was slightly ashamed of her attitude towards him now, beginning to feel just a little uneasy about it. And as for her lifelong craving for so-called respectability, well, if she were absolutely truthful, she'd have to say that while her aspiration towards it had been comforting, it had in the end simply evaded her, and she had to ask why.

Recently, during a spell of very hot weather, the long unbroken rhythm of Robert Radnor's life began to falter. To begin with, it was the heat. Normally it wouldn't have worried him much, but this time, it was quite beyond his melting point. It prevented sleep. And the thick membrane which he'd consciously grown and which hindered any sensitive touch or caress with certain memories, began to dissolve. He had not experienced such temperatures since his days on the Burma run before the war, but now it seemed as if it was actually melting those petrified, lost memories so long forgotten, so that they moved again in his mind, threatening to undermine him and all that had supported him for so long.

Without sleep his mind began to drift, he ate little and finally became ill. He wandered about in a delirium, getting weaker, hallucinating, sensing the ground at last falling away, seeing himself within his tiny ambit and the patterns of what he began to see as piles of junk, and himself again, lost, prospecting for all the world's leavings.

His illness left him one day below the tideline, naked, lying face up to the sun, his arms and legs stretched wide, like some kind of ritual sacrifice. The soupy water of the incoming tide was already halfway up his legs when he was found. With his long hair fanned out around his head, full of sand and seaweed, he could have been Neptune himself washed up on the shore.

This was not the first time in his life he'd been found close to death on a beach.

The few days he spent in hospital were barely supportable. There were patients everywhere, and staff talking at him incessantly, talk which he found impossible to consider. When he did try to respond, he either forgot what he was saying in what people took to be his shyness, or became so unwilling that his voice was reduced to a murmur. When he looked about from his hospital bed, at the other patients and at the diligent, hard-working nurses, he felt more acutely than ever the absurdity in everything. Yet he remembered that the writing of his book had been a laborious undertaking, one to which, at the time, he had wholly committed himself. And it had after all allowed him to retreat into a life of his own choosing. Of course it was also true that his solitary life had then been exposed to the measured development of a sharper, more insidious kind of anguish which had been the direct result of his not living up to his own beliefs. He knew this to be so, knew in his heart in a way that only he could, that he had once cheated the Sea. Yet he had lived.

Sitting up in the folds of his white hospital bed, his long

hair falling about his shoulders, he bowed his head towards his hands.

After so many years of solitude, attempts by the nurses and others to engage him in some kind of exchange would provoke strange responses. He would shuffle his feet uncomfortably, sending currents of unease throughout his body. With one stained and knotted hand he would knead the loose skin around his mouth and jaw, his face contorting before he could utter one single word. The effort seemed titanic, and in the end fruitless. Or he would simply lie back and curse, fighting off any kind of assistance. Even so, in the end he was accommodated at the hospital, tolerated, because it was believed his experiences at sea had turned his mind.

One night soon after his return home, he woke up, again deeply troubled by his memories. He knew no one, no one came, it had been what he'd wanted, always, but now to have a friend, someone on the level, that was what he wanted above all else. Perhaps then he would be able to break the silence. But he had locked himself in so completely, so effectively insulated himself from the world, bought his own exile at a price unspecified, that now he had something he must say, he could not. He swung his legs out of bed and sat for a moment looking across his cluttered burrow to the open veranda window. Outside the night was silvery from the full moon, the tide was making, and beyond earshot, beyond the concentration of light at Felixstowe docks, in a confused sea of wind against tide, the plump bows of a freighter rolled before it a brilliant white moustache of phosphorescence. Radnor placed his elbows on his knees, and his hands, which he seemed to study, he turned about in the dim light, letting them hang limply between his legs, weighing them up as if they were objects that didn't belong to him. All round the room, barely discernible, placed on every conceivable horizontal surface were the products of these hands, the Puckish figures he spent his winters carving. He knew them all, knew their places in time, remembered the moments of their particular creation. In the winter he would sit shaving the wood until it was time for sleep. His memory had always threatened to turn sour on him, and at night when the problem seemed worse, he defended himself against it by carving an army.

But now, finally, with precarious age and frailty, his guard was finally coming down.

He struggled to his feet and stayed stooping, suspended, looking out across the river, looking into it, as if trying to divine something. On the far bank the lights of a car flickered through the trees, sending brief serpentine reflections across the water. Radnor thought of the place dried up, the steep banks leading down to the sluiced channel bed with its pebbles dry and white, and all the fish and tiny creatures, feathery and blown about on the baked surface. He thought of the enforced weeks on the Indian coast during the monsoons, waiting to load jute, and the sea snakes, like spaghetti there were so many, and the sticky night breeze, and his longing for the open sea, and then the rusting ship, grimy and incongruous in the deep blue of the ocean.

Before he moved again the ship which had been approaching the mouth of the river was nearing that place in the water into which he stared transfixed. Its passing, with a thunder of engines and purpose and aglow with lights, broke the spell and he returned from where he'd been, watching the ship with a sharp critical gaze until it had gone.

Turning away, he whispered something into the darkness, then coughed repeatedly, fighting to gain breath, the veins standing out on his neck like ropes. So close to the end, he understood he would at last be doing Her bidding, that now finally, the courses and drift of his life, for so long denied, were demanding reconciliation.

Not long after this, Radnor was sitting on the wooden steps of his veranda reading and cutting himself tiny morsels of the apple he'd picked from the ancient hedgerow, which grew wild as barbed wire along the track. From time to time, he combed long strands of hair away from his face with his fingers, and looked out towards the boats fidgeting at their moorings. It was almost high water.

He was reading a battered old hardback held together with tape, flicking through it, stopping and re-reading, then going on and back and forth, finally closing the book, purposefully, almost reverently, as though it were a book of prayer. He shut his eyes, drawing in a full lungful of air. For a few moments he remained still, then as he opened his eyes, he flung the book, flapping like an injured bird, out on to the sloppy sand at the water's edge.

'There's a beginning of an end to it,' he croaked. He sat quite still, watching, as the last of the tide licked at the book, lifting it a little further up the beach. Radnor hung his head. He might have been asleep, or dead.

'You all right, sir?'
The young man's voice seemed a long way off, yet it might have come from inside his own skull. It was an odd kind of congruence this, yet it wasn't. It was no more than he expected; a sychronising of things towards a particular point. He'd been thinking how once, as mate of the *Golden Delta*, a younger officer had joined him on the fo'c'sle head with almost the same words.

Radnor looked round. A young man was standing close to the inland corner of the shack. He was still, watching, coming no nearer. He was dressed in that uniform of sensible, country clothing which nevertheless sanctions certain flourishes of *élan*, and might appear as a pair of carroty coloured trousers or a lemon waistcoat, setting off subdued country tweeds with a splash of colour. In his case it was a strawberry waistcoat, and an enormous silk handkerchief ballooning from his top pocket.

'You all right, sir?' he said again.

Radnor pulled himself to his feet. The boy must have climbed over the gate. People didn't seem to be deterred so much these days. From force of habit he felt his lungs fill against the intrusion, felt himself about to roar. But then something prevented it, and he stared impassively at the young man who had already retreated a couple of paces.

'Mr Radnor? It is Mr Radnor, isn't it?'

Now the old man began to conjure up his voice, rocking from side to side, stroking his beard, clearing his throat, coughing. But when it came to it, his throat tightened and he began again to cough and choke. Finally, with another attempt, thumping his chest with his fist, he said, barely audible, wheezing out the words, 'Why shouldn't I be all right? What do you want?'

The young man came forward. 'My name's . . .' He stopped, then came closer, holding out his hand. 'My name's Jeremy Thomson.'

Radnor made no response. He was brimming with suspicion.

'I'm the land agent for Major Wilkes.'

The old man didn't appear to hear him.

'Major Wilkes,' Jeremy Thomson repeated, as though it were some kind of password.

'I heard you.'

Cracked and hoarse though it was, Radnor's voice was now suddenly stronger.

'Major Wilkes. Yes. What does he want?'

13

At this point he stretched out an enormous hand towards his visitor, who went to take it. But there was an ambiguity in the move, and Radnor grabbed the veranda rail instead, to steady himself.

'Not here,' he said, 'not . . . here. Not . . . now.' He stood looking at the boy, waving him away before he shuffled towards the door, adroitly flicking it shut as he passed through. There was a ringing metallic clunk as the bolt was drawn sharply across.

Ever since he'd first arrived at Hevingbroke, Radnor had rented his home for a peppercorn from the local farmer, who'd always express (on their rare meetings) a certain kindly magnanimity which had never failed to check Radnor's loss of nerve. He'd heard recently of the old fellow's death. He'd have been about the same age as Radnor himself. And now he'd already begun to feel his loss more than he once might have expected. Perhaps at the back of his mind he'd seen him as some sort of confessor. Radnor knew he'd been the one man who might have been able to listen, and the one man whom Radnor might have been able to trust. But in the gloom of his shack, with this 'land agent' outside, his friend's passing came home to him with a shock he'd not expected.

The changes on the farm had been immediate and plain to see. New tractors, new faces, but most of all a frenetic impatience in place of steady, indomitable labour. Life was changing all around him, and one day soon, he knew he too would be part of it.

Radnor sank into his chair, and gave a shudder. For the first time in over forty-five years, since he'd crept into this corner of the world, he felt forces converging on him once again.

★　　★　　★

Some minutes passed, until, there being no sound from outside, Radnor heaved himself up from his chair and went to the window. The boy was still there. 'Blast!' he muttered. 'Fuck 'im.'

Jeremy Thomson stood just outside, chewing his bottom lip. His knuckles were poised at that very moment, about to rap at the door, when out of the corner of his eye he caught sight of the old man staring at him.

'Mr Radnor!'

Radnor jerked his head away from the window and stood for a moment considering the position. Moving silently through the gloom, he quietly unbolted the door, swung it open, and shambled out into the sun.

'I'm sorry if I'm causing you a problem, Mr Radnor,' the young man said, getting straight back into it, 'but this really is quite important. If I could just have five minutes of your time to show you these —' he waved a sheaf of papers before him — 'that's all it would take. Perhaps we might go inside?'

Radnor grunted something, shook his head in exasperation, and reluctantly led the way back inside.

Gazing about in the dark little refuge, Jeremy Thomson was physically stopped by what he saw.

The whole place was carved. Carvings everywhere. Hundreds. Even the wooden walls themselves hadn't been spared. There didn't seem to be a square inch that hadn't received the same treatment. Chairs, table, shelves, everything. And there were countless individual carvings too, lining the shelves, small faces turned towards the centre of the room, where there were two disintegrating armchairs. Many of these faces were disquieting, their expressions penetrating. And with some there was an emptiness, like a plain mask until an actor gives it force.

Radnor went over to his seat and sat silently staring at

the ground, at home with the strange figures, but cowed by this young presence.

'These are extraordinary!' Jeremy Thomson burst out after a long silence.

Radnor looked up from under a heavy, hooded frown, having heard not so much the words as the tone, then, returning his gaze to the floor, placing his elbows on his knees and his head between his hands, he mumbled almost inaudibly, 'Let's get on with it then.'

Jeremy Thomson edged towards the other chair, looking about him all the while. His earlier 'amazement' was now begetting a more genuine interest. He stood in the centre of the room, feet firmly planted, confident of what he repre-sented, one hand thrust deep into his pocket jingling coins, the other holding documents to his chest, regarding the gallery of heads, which he now realised extended to parts of the roof as well. He was wondering whether they'd be worth anything, these carvings, especially those little heads, whether there'd be a market for them. He'd never seen anything quite like them. They were rather wonderful. Intense. Frightening in a way. He never knew he could be moved by such things.

Radnor lifted his eyes again to catch the young man examining the roof beams, then running his fingers over the smoothed grooves in the faces on the shelves, violating his innermost privacies. And there in that instant, frozen in his mind, Radnor saw the perfidious nature of his visitor.

But it was a while before he reacted. Jeremy Thomson reached the armchair and, with a silken movement, sat down, a broad grin spreading across a tidy face.

'Now then, Mr Radnor, I'll come straight to the point.' He riffled through his papers. 'Yes, here we are. You see, there doesn't appear to be any record . . .' he looked up, 'of rents. We've got your original agreement here, but there's no mention of, as I say, rents. Seems rather odd.' There was a pause while he watched Radnor, who still gazed at the floor. 'Anyway, I'm sure you'll understand. Major Wilkes would like to get things put on a proper footing and . . . Mr Radnor?'

But it was plain Radnor had not been listening. He was somewhere else. In fact, the young man thought, he seemed a bit lacking. Now this, of course, could make the world of difference. Make the job considerably easier, he thought. A nutcase, and an old nutcase living down here on his own. The social services would certainly have something to say about that. And then the matter might be taken out of his hands altogether. A good thing! He began to sense his problem solved.

The old man was still not moving. He didn't appear to have heard anything.

As Jeremy Thomson looked on he persuaded himself that Mr Radnor's eviction might actually come to be viewed in a favourable light. A responsible move by the Wilkes Partnership! Though either way, he reflected, people being what they are, Radnor and his shack would be long forgotten by the time any development actually started.

There was silence, as if in that time between the specious patter of a grenade's arrival and its detonation. Radnor, having lifted his head at last, was gazing distantly at nothing.

The old man began to struggle to his feet, as though his life depended on it. There was a rumbling from somewhere deep in his chest and he rose, lifting his arms out sideways, and with the palms of his great hands like paddles, waved the young man away, roaring at him, 'Gorworn! Out! Gorworn with yer. Out of here!'

At first, Jeremy Thomson could not comprehend what was happening. He couldn't move, couldn't turn his mind around from courteous dominance to naked survival in so short a space. He retreated deeper into his chair. There were stalactites of saliva trembling between Radnor's lips as he roared on over him. 'Gorworn!' That huge head over him, against the carved roof of the shack. There was no time. He gathered everything up as best he could, papers slicing to the ground, scrambling out of his chair, tripping, crawling, racing for the open door. Once outside, he ran as hard as he could through the sunshine, out along the shoreline, sheaves of paper motoring at his chest, his tie fluttering over his shoulder. Turning on the run, in a panic of speed he caught sight of Radnor's book lifted further up the beach by the dying eddies of the flood tide. A little further on, at what he gauged to be a safe distance, he stopped to catch his breath and looked back.

Radnor emerged, carefully negotiating the steps, and stood at the bottom, back against the rail, chest heaving. He was smiling, nodding his head in confirmation of something.

Jeremy Thomson noticed a little too late a sweep of the tide which just covered his shoes, the water seeping through to his socks and making him jump as if he'd been bitten. It gave him the impetus to shout back at Radnor, 'What they say about you is true.' He wanted to say more, and as he regained his breath, with each heave of his chest it looked as though he might, but he only stared in turmoil.

The two of them stood facing each other on the shore, Radnor's face twisted down, and Jeremy Thomson slowly regained his composure, his confidence flowing back with the one thought in his head, that here indeed was a clear case for the social services. Radnor saw the change in the young man's posture as he stood there. He was not mistaken, and he unbuttoned his trousers and peed then and there into the dry sand. Afterwards he climbed back up the steps to lean on the rail as though he were completely alone, his gaze following the course of the river to the sea.

After a time, Jeremy Thomson walked shakily over to the book lying in the wet sand and bent to pick it up. There was only a part of the dust jacket remaining, with the words ROBERT RADNOR blazoned in what had once been white lettering across a dark and stormy sea. Inside, on the relatively untouched part of the cover was a photograph of the author, unmistakable, which he studied before lifting his eyes in a slow, absorbing arc towards the steps and the now empty veranda.

Jeremy Thomson had to circle around through the trees to get back to his car without being spotted. He could not believe what had happened. He kept seeing the old man roaring at him from above as he'd sat in that filthy old chair. It had brought on, just for a moment or two, a disarrangement of his own private, familiar world, the way he looked at things – immutable relations, language, routine, the bedrock of certain knowledge. Things he just knew, and relied on. The unquestioning acceptance of the world into which he had been born. It was a momentary derailing or – he could not bear to think – a flaying. He thought of war, innocence, and when hands join in some profane rite. All these things flashing into his mind. Why should they? He began to run, attributing it to Mr Radnor, seeing the old man as some kind of sorcerer, exerting strange, discomforting influences on him. And those heads, he felt their penetrating gaze again as he clasped the book, trotting through the trees, breathless at the threatening havoc of his own imagination, head down, holding on to his familiar world by concentrating on his expensive brogues squelching water at every step, the sound of his quick breathing muffled by the soft floor of the wood, his legs heavy, sensing a pursuer, an ever-watching eye.

Once he'd reached his car, he locked himself in, running

his hand lovingly around the expensive wooden steering wheel. The obedient ignition, the murmuring engine, the familiar smell, were like tiny seeds which grew into the entire, symmetrical summer garden of his even life. It was there again, reassuringly, every part of it. His. But he had been shaken by the depth of his fear, and by an imagination he never knew he possessed, nor indeed wanted, and this he began to think, as the car at last left the tumbling track for the road, was like an appalling virus, activated by that old man and his inscrutable carvings.

On his way back to the office, he decided to call at the village post office. He'd called there earlier, but Mrs Morrow had been very cagey when it came to the subject of Mr Radnor. He'd learnt he was 'difficult'. Nothing else. Now, after his visit, he wanted to plant a seed.

He found her on her own, leaning on the counter, reading a newspaper.

'Well,' she said. 'Did you find him?'

With his well-worked technique of balancing confidence with self-effacement, he said, 'I have to admit, there is something in what you said.'

'What did I say?'

'You said I might find him rather strange.'

'And did you?'

'Yes.'

'Well, as I said, he's not fond of people.'

'No.'

There was a pause.

'It's none of my business, but why would anybody want to go and see him anyway? He's lived there so many years now and no one's ever gone to see him that I know of.'

Another pause. She looked at him. 'My guess is you're something to do with this, aren't you?' She spun the newspaper around on the counter and pointed to a short article under the heading FREIGHTER FOUND.

He picked up the paper and read:

Divers have discovered the remains of the British freighter *Golden Delta*, which foundered in the Bay of Bengal in 1949. It has caused some bafflement in shipping circles since her location on the western extremity of the Andaman Islands does not correspond to that given at the subsequent inquest by her chief officer and sole survivor. The inconsistency was restated later in a book about the tragedy written by the same man. Further inquiries are expected.

He read it carefully, shaking his head. 'I don't understand.'

'That's him, isn't it? That was his ship. I heard he'd written a book or something.'

Jeremy Thomson slid his hand into his side pocket and pulled out the book, like a conjuror, holding it up without a word.

'Where did you find that?' asked Mrs Morrow, stretching out her hand to take it.

'On the beach.'

'On the beach!'

'Just outside his . . . shack.'

'May I have a look?'

He handed it to her.

'So this is it.' She turned the pages without reading. 'I've heard about this. Never seen a copy. My God . . . you can see it's him.' She turned the book. 'I'd like to read this.'

'I'll lend it to you. When I've finished with it.' He held out his hand to take it back, then dropped it into his pocket. 'By the way,' he said, pausing till he had regained all her attention, 'you wouldn't happen to know who his doctor is?'

'His doctor!' She laughed.

Mrs Morrow's voice had the unmistakable note of the proprietor. Protective against this outside current of curiosity. Because of her traditional animosity towards the old man, and her recent feeling of guilt about it, she found herself needing to know exactly what was happening where he was concerned. It seemed he'd taken up lodging in her imagination. This was her domain, and someone was trespassing. She crossed her arms. 'You know, Mr Radnor has always minded his own business. Why should someone suddenly want to mind his?'

'Oh I'm sorry, I should have told you. I'm the land agent for the Wilkes Partnership at Hevingbroke Hall. Church Farm?'

She nodded.

'Well, as the land agent I have the job of looking after tenants. That includes Mr Radnor, I'm afraid.'

'So why the doctor?'

'Simply a matter of keeping an eye on him. He's old. I'm not sure he's that well either. We have a responsibility.'

'Oh yes?'

'Yes!'

'He seemed all right to me when I saw him. I should think I'd have more idea than anyone how he is. Anyway I thought that old place was his.'

'I have to tell you the whole of Garden Reach . . . from the point as far as the old track, is owned by Church Farm. I don't think many people realise that.'

A pause.

'Well,' Mrs Morrow said, 'I think you should ask him who his doctor is. Doesn't seem right. He likes to be left alone. He's sort of a hermit. Hates visitors.'

Jeremy Thomson smiled. A patronising smile. As though there were things she would just never understand.

She pursed her lips. 'I'll give that book back to him

if you like,' she said, nodding towards his pocket.

He hesitated and shook his head. 'That's OK. I'll do it.' He looked at his watch. 'My God look at the time! Thanks for your help.' And before she could say anything, he'd gone.

'Help. What help?' she said, coming round to the front of the counter, her gaze attracted by the rectangle of blue sky at the top of the doorway, so much in contrast to the dingy confinement of the shop. She felt a pulse of urgency to go down and see Mr Radnor, to warn him. But about what?

She sighed and went to stand by the door. A breeze had begun to blow through the shop. She let it ruffle her hair, enjoying its feathery touch, holding her head back, closing her eyes, taking in a long, deep draught. She stayed there for a moment in the sunlight.

It was odd how Mr Radnor, having been on her mind so much just recently, now seemed to be on everyone else's too. It was as though the world had suddenly caught up with him, this old man who'd lived with his secrets on the edge of her community for so long.

She returned to the dimness of the shop where she was brought up short by the sight of herself in the mirror. Standing squarely before it, faint reflected light picking out threads of silver in her dark hair, she thought the familiar lines in her face looked deeper than she remembered. Age had crept up under the trance of familiarity. She frowned her respectability and thought her features fell into the expression all too easily. It frightened her this, as though − had she wanted it − she had left too late any notion of escape.

Far out in the ocean, there are places where everything seems at odds, the ship lurches through a bewitched world of pointed hills, the constant even divisions of marching waves break up, wind dies, and the ship's movement is no longer predictable. Then, occasionally − a *coup de grâce*! A tiny impulse for whatever cause, perhaps at the furthest depths, starts a sequence – little surges unite attracting others with split-second timing, heaving upwards together, growing, synchronising, gathering power all the while, until at last a vast invisible mass of water, fed by a hundred confluences, erupts, discharging its energies against the air – a monstrous wave which we must expediently call freak.

Radnor knew it all by heart. He'd gone over the words, written so long ago, a thousand times, unable to forget them. But as always he was tormented by the truth within the lie.

'Like attracts like! That's all there is to it.'

Radnor submitted to it, boiled the kettle, made a port-hole in the steamed-up window, and peered through.

What did he know? He knew that once things were synchronised, as they were now, there was no telling how large the 'freak' might grow. But that thought did not terrorise him as it once had. The force which his secreted, half-forgotten knowledge was exerting upwards into the light was undeni-able, and the thought of its emergence at long last into the sunshine of his ninety-fourth summer filled him with a kind of hope, a faith even, because he knew with a fatalism he once would have fought that there was no controlling it, that it would out in its own way, in its own time, according to whichever laws. It was only that, before that happened, he wished to make his secret known, to acknowledge it out loud with his own voice, in front of someone before he died.

He made some coffee and went to resume his musings on the steps. It was the other story he now had to face, to learn again – the one waiting behind the familiar.

Radnor appeared at his door. He was dragging a heavy sack towards the veranda steps. There he stopped, out of breath, raising his head to look across the sliding river. A heavy branch sailed past on the ebb, one valedictory limb thrown high; a gull flapped clumsily around alighting for a second on the very tip of its bony finger, capsizing it, the sun penetrating the dark underwater caverns of weed. He bumped the sack down on to the shingly sand, stood a little uncertainly, watching, then sat on the steps in his usual position – elbows on knees, feet wide, and as a stay of execution allowed himself for a second or two the pleasure of a fine morning. This was the moment he had buried for so long. The moment he never considered he would meet, especially in the conscious way he now did. Where to begin? How to begin? He was being shoved and jostled towards it, helpless. He laughed as in defence, then dropped his head, closing his eyes, rubbing them with the curve of his forefingers, like the little boy so long ago. A strange kind of thing, that. He would run along in the playground and stop, suddenly jumping on to both feet, and bend down squinting earnestly at the ground, rubbing his eyes as if he were trying to see something, but never could. Then he would run on and do it again, and again, all round the playground. What was it about? No one asked. Perhaps they knew. He was sinking back, returning now to the beginning. Lowering himself into a bath of memories. The older they are, the more vivid. Radnor rocked back and forth, his eyes still closed, his head down. 'Strange little boy.'

He shifted his feet, and in the boundless reaches beyond the capes saw the whale rolling over and over, never seeming to come to the end of itself – a giant black ball rolling on for ever. There were places in the ocean that seemed to possess their own definite identities – the ship would steam into them and through them and during that time these places would communicate: melancholy, hope, birth, exuberance, despair – he had always been susceptible to them. They would, living, penetrate and govern him for the time. The endless empty sea. No more than that? It had been his deepening sense of these invisible frontiers, and later sometimes his presentiment of them that turned him into a fine instinctive seaman, instincts all too absent in the modern world.

A gust of wind pushed along the shore, bringing a chill not felt for months, the first volley of autumn rattling the leaves, and he understood that there could be no more winters. He would not want to see another winter, if it were now no longer necessary to defend himself with his carving.

But against what? Whatever it was, now, finally, he had had to stop running from it. It seemed to have caught up with him at last. He felt its closeness, but it was not touching him, not yet. It was stationary, near him, waiting with the consideration and dominion of a courteous torturer, giving him time, just a little more time. He recognised it of course, prepared himself, and in due course there came a sound like deep lowing laughter, as he wept.

He sat in the same position for an hour, his eyes fixed like a snake's. Then he went and rummaged in the sack, urgently, as though time enough had passed and he could delay things no longer. Picking over the carved heads, he stared into them, lost in thought, before hurling them out with sudden youthful energy into the ebb stream, watching them bob in procession towards the sea – friends, relatives, seamen, his life sculpted from his earliest memories. And so he worked down the stations of the years, running through them one final time. When he'd finished lobbing them into the stream, when the sack was empty, he sat with the sounds of the trees and the life of the uncovering mud and the slackening tide now out of range.

The next day and the next, he pulled out his sacks full of memories, and the coconut-sized heads, once so valuable, were jettisoned into the outgoing tide. At the back of his mind, what he was doing reminded him of someone, but the memory wouldn't come. Meanwhile the sackloads were emptied, the heads cast out to float away, and all the time memories renewed and set free. Each day another crop made the journey towards the sea.

Some of these heads had started out as random carvings of no one in particular, but it was never how they ended up. If there had been no one in his mind at the outset, there would always be someone there later. It was as if his hands really had not belonged to him, but were working to someone else's commands.

They were noticed of course, these little heads, bobbing about in the currents, first by the fishermen who threw them back with the fish entrails, and then by the yachtsmen in their shining yachts. Among this group of people the word spread rapidly, and although no one knew what they were, or where they came from, there was something which said they might conceivably have some worth. And even if it turned out this were not so, there was still value in the mystery. It prompted a spontaneous and fierce competition, where expensive yachts cut in and out like martins catching insects on the wind. A few people began to assemble quite a collection. In time, the heads were dried and polished and found their way on to market stalls and into curio shops. Amongst a few they were prized and traded at ever increasing prices. Locally they were known as the Orwell Heads, their reputation widening as their value grew.

Radnor was not aware of the attention they were attracting, only that the greater powers were focusing on him, and his every breath. He accepted it, as he always had, asking nothing, but hearing once more the clear calling from so long ago. Then one day he found himself staring into the face of his old German camp commandant and he remembered what it was he had been reminded of. The cherubic face of this young German officer, the high puffy cheeks and slanting almost oriental eyes that seemed always to be secretly entertained and yet determinedly seeing nothing, had been fashioned from a piece of apple wood. This man, who had interviewed him with such amused curiosity on his first day as a prisoner of war, stared up from his cupped hand across fifty-three years.

Radnor had survived a torpedo attack in the Sicilian Channel and had been taken to a German holding camp just outside Carthage to await transport; transport that for Radnor at least was never needed. He escaped, and in a tiny fishing boat, alone, and after an extraordinarily easy journey, arrived safely in Malta. It was like all the memories he had renewed so far – a real memory – in it he had trust, it was unassailable and it finally brought to mind what it was he couldn't remember. What had been nothing before, darkness, was now a memory more vivid than all the others.

The makeshift holding camp had been arranged on a farm, and the position of the pound where the prisoners were housed made it possible to look through the wire, across the stack yard, to an area of open ground at the rear of the farmhouse. Just beyond the back door of the house, in the shade of a eucalyptus tree, the French farmer set up a table from which he dispensed the wages on Friday evenings. It wasn't the religious feel of the line of subdued workers shuffling along in silent humility which interested Radnor, nor how much they all seemed, as they stepped forward with supplicatory bows, to revere their master, it was more what happened afterwards that impressed him. Always at this time, a group of children appeared, high spirited beyond their awareness of the occupying soldiers, and they gathered on the open ground close to a straw stack, playing in the dust and the cool of the long shadow it made. As the workers melted away, a towering man, always the last to collect his money, distinguished also by a natural grace and easy security, wandered grinning and on the point of laughter towards the children. This man, his face made almost featureless by the distance at which Radnor watched, and by his coal black skin, sauntered amongst the children, brushing their heads tenderly with the palms of his hands and laughing softly, the pockets of the sound melting and low, ferrying over the evening air towards the pound. There must have been a ladder on the other side of the stack, for very quickly he was up and standing on top of it – roaring with laughter now at the excited children below, who were beginning to shout up to him delightedly and impatiently. With painful deliberation, to extract more squeals, he began to toss coins down to them, so that they scavenged about in the dusty soil, rushing from one spot to another like birds after crumbs. He threw away his wages like this, always taking it in coin of the lowest denomination. It was a weekly theatre which brought smiles to the faces of the most heartless of the guards.

But who was this benefactor, and why did he do it? Among the secrets and rumour there was something everyone knew. He lived in a shack he had built for himself not far from the main complex of buildings which constituted the farm village, worked hard and was kept in clothes, food and tobacco by the grateful farmer. He had, it was said, spent his life as a Nubian slave. Whether he had escaped or been officially granted his freedom and how he came to be there, nothing and no one could induce him to say. Radnor understood that the depth of something or its intensity is made possible only by an equal understanding of its opposite, that the man's freedom, the freeness of it, grew only from the deep established root of his own slavery. Of the man's head Radnor oddly had no carving, only the memory – the curls of pipe smoke from where he sat outside his shack looking steadfastly towards the pound, warm empty evenings, the flat arid ground between, and the encircling wire.

Radnor went on in this manner retracing his life, until he reached those post-war years when he had served as chief officer on the steamship *Golden Delta*. It was after she had foundered in the Bay of Bengal in November 1949 that he had returned home to such publicity, and it was these times which now began to fill his mind. He reached up for the head of the ship's master, the lugubrious Archibald Peeke, complete with pipe and his regrets still about him, that he ever followed a sea life, not becoming a farmer like his brother. And those of the quartermasters, Evans and Murphy, and the chief engineer Angus McIver, a squat pugnacious man with ever the single conclusive word on all things, all now exposed and gazing down from the depleted but so recently crowded shelves. Radnor picked them from their places and put them on the table, arranging them so that they all faced each other – heads which had, with others from the ship's company, haunted him for so long. All dead. Not one of them surviving. And there was that block of lime wood, blank, which was to have been some kind of self-portrait, but which he could never bring himself to carve. For he was not one of them. Nor was he a survivor. Certainly he'd gone on living since then, he'd breathed, but his life had been stretched out so thinly and for so long, you could barely see it. It had not really been a life, but then how could he have gone on at sea knowing what it was the Sea demanded? Even now on the river, in his skiff, he could feel the 'pull', as he called it, the clear calling. His intuition had survived outside of the modern world with its greed for data; it had been learned from the Sea, and like the gift of healing, did not bear logic or illogic. He had taken it, learnt it, it had saved him, but in the process, he had betrayed it.

Now along with the courage he was able to call up to face these things, came a recognisable spirit, a deep knowledge, once again, as he prowled in his mind along the decks of the *Golden Delta*, hearing again the ringing metallic sounds of the ship, passing the expressions of men reacting to something he also then remembered, building up the world of the ship in complementary multiples, until he actually stood as near as dammit on her well deck, boat deck, bridge deck – alive, standing, watching – a phantom with a world going on all around. Could they see him? Could any of them have had any sense of the place and time from which he now watched them?

This was his last voyage, the last days, as he now considered them to be, of his life – his time since then becoming somehow illicit.

THREE

H E WAS THEN in his mid-forties and getting on in years for a chief officer, but the Delta Line of Liverpool was a small, friendly company of only six ships, commanding loyalty from the crews, and after his wartime experiences, a cosy security. Their ships were well built and comfortable, the feeding excellent, and so too the money, and one had the feeling of being looked after. No one with any sense would give up a berth on a Delta boat, so it was a case of waiting for dead men's shoes, which did not bother Radnor, for though he had not acknowledged it, he had somewhere and at some time let go his belief that he was a lifelong mariner. The years of war had left him mistrustful. Nothing changed. Nor ever would. No frantic work and planning and scurrying about the globe and industry and struggle, had any relevance any more. For him it was absurd, all of it.

The company did not operate a regular liner service. They were tramp steamers picking up cargoes wherever they could and going where the trade took them. Sometimes they were away for years at a stretch, blown around the world by the winds of whatever trade could be found. It did not matter to Radnor; he had no family left, had never married, never wanted to marry, although he had an affectionate heart and spent much of his life craving and often buying the affections of women – the world over. He had felt deserted when, at the age of twelve, his mother had died, the sense of being quite alone and the need to love and be loved never so poignantly felt than when he first went to sea. But in due course, he learnt to understand that he was in another's company only in so far as he believed everyone else to be alone, unable to escape their own solitary state. For him, any other thought was vanity.

This last voyage had been unusual in that the ship had had orders from northern European ports to India, and thence from India, Burma and Pakistan straight back home again – the round voyage extending to no more than eight or nine months. But there'd been problems of one sort or another from the start, and there'd been talk of a Jonah on board. First, they'd been delayed in London by a dockers' strike, ill-fortune seeming to follow the ship from then on. Delay after delay. And when, finally, they had broken free of northern Europe, on a blustery day in the Bay the main drive shaft had failed, badly injuring one of the engineers, and ending with a difficult tow in heavy seas into Lorient.

Radnor had been in charge of the party on the fo'c'sle head and having once secured the tow and stood the crew down, he himself seemed entranced by the whole operation – the powerful little tug and the hawser singing with the strain. It was a dangerous place to be and it was not long before a wet and nervous apprentice arrived at his side.

'Captain says to stand down . . . now sir . . . please.'

Far worse happened a day or two later, in the Mediterranean, at about the place Radnor had crossed in the fishing boat, after his escape from Carthage. A warning, he vaguely felt afterwards, that recent thoughts he'd been having about leaving the sea might be known. Perhaps to the Sea herself.

And having so assuredly granted him much luck in the past, bestowing that rare gift of intuition upon him, might she not forbid his desertion? This, in his growing isolation, is what he privately feared. The incident happened in bad weather during a particularly sudden and savage squall. The serang had been turning down a mushroom ventilator on the fo'c'sle head, his form clinging, bent like the round back of a flea and the ship lunging about like a lassoed mustang, when suddenly he was seen detached, rising high above the bows, a tiny figure against the sea, turning slowly in the air, hanging there as the deck dropped thirty feet from under him and as quickly shot up to meet his fall, halving his head against a steel stanchion. With the next heel of the ship, as easy as pouring lumpy soup, he was emptied into the sea. At about the same time, below, one of the junior cooks had placed a long kitchen knife unchocked on a work surface, and went to open a cool room on the other side of the galley. As he turned to come back, the ship, recovering from a strangely deep roll, forced him against the doors he had just closed and, so pinioned, the knife lifted and guided as if by an invisible hand spun around and streaked through the beaten air, piercing his eye, driving itself far into his brain. The two deaths occurred more or less at the same place.

Of course Radnor couldn't talk about his fears, about this presence, this jealous presence to whom he owed his life, they'd think him mad, but he felt it with a keener edge than he sensed say, bad weather, or danger in the offing, or the proximity of a whale, these things not known exactly as he now knew, but situated somewhere between consciousness and unconsciousness. He was relieved when the bad weather passed through and they had left behind the intersection of his two courses.

As they approached the Suez Canal and shallower waters,

he felt the waning of his own sharp seagoing instincts, and fell to practising seamanship, pilotage and navigation by the book, his relationship with Captain Peeke and the other officers becoming more open – and this deep sea fluence, this knowing which sometimes simply took hold of him, creating as it did a certain tension between the clear facts of a case and what his intuition told him, had gone.

Now and for a little while he was blessedly like everybody else. But although, during their canal transit, he would feel no more such influences, they were never far from him, nor could he forget the strong forebodings that had possessed him as he stood entranced on the fo'c'sle head at the time of the tow into Lorient, and the revelation, as he had watched the lethal snatching hawser, that he was really no longer free, if he ever had been, but seduced, drawn along by some other masked power.

From the after rail of the boat deck, where he liked to plant his chair after dark, Radnor could watch the intermittent glow of Captain Peeke's pipe as he paced the bridge.

This was the captain's habit at sea for perhaps two hours every evening, before retiring below for his lukewarm gin and water taken from a toothmug. Sometimes, a little later, he'd go down to Radnor's cabin for a game of chess and a chat.

That night was hot and brilliant, and the ship's roll – but for the gentle movement of night shade across the deck – barely perceptible, the steam turbine exhaling from the towering black funnel in one never-ending breath.

If he could have seen Captain Peeke's features, Radnor would have beheld what he himself imagined at that moment: his long face drawn as if from two points on either side of his mouth, two little knotted fists of muscle pulling all downward so that his bottom eyelids showed red, and if, as Radnor thought he might be, he was thinking how it was that he was nearing the end of his career without ever making that change he'd so often dreamt of, his eyes would be bulging slightly in an expression of doleful paralysis, held there and fixed by the pipe thrust between his teeth.

There was a muddle of shipping away on the starboard hand at some distance, heading north. Radnor knew that soon Archibald Peeke would confirm the night order book and reluctantly leave the third mate, a young and inexperienced officer, to his watch. But on this night the pipe continued its rhythmic journeying a little longer. The old man was no doubt nervous about the young officer in these narrow seas. Radnor smiled and looked up at the sky. Because the stars were especially bright, he had the idea that he was looking up inside a vast rusting wartime helmet, through countless little holes which were letting in the brilliance from some other universe.

He got up from his chair and sauntered across the cambered deck to the port rail, then began to retrace his steps. As he went, he faltered, feeling shadowed by a familiar intuition which presaged some kind of change. It was a feeling he knew well, advancing a challenge, a dare not to recognise it before some imminent variation in the normal course of things. Lately these feelings, always bending his attention towards the sea where sometimes he had seen strange forms swimming beside the ship, had become stronger.

Years before, when he'd been a junior apprentice, there was a game they'd played at sea. They, the apprentices – normally three or four of them – would gather on the after deck just before dark. It was more of an initiation by trial than a game. The idea was to hang over the stern, fingers curled over the steel lip at the edge of the deck, nothing between them and certain death. The winner was simply the one hanging on by the least number of fingers. It was an absurdly dangerous thing to do, and it was during one of these contests that Radnor had very nearly let go. It would have been nothing for him to hang on for minutes at a time, but on this occasion he'd found himself rapidly, inexplicably, losing his strength. The senior apprentice, one Archibald Peeke, had saved him in the end, grabbing him at the very last moment and only just managing to haul him back on board. It had been such a shock to all of them they'd never played the game again. For some reason Radnor had found he couldn't speak, let alone cry out. He'd felt his throat constricted, as if small hands had joined around it. There was also something about the experience he'd never mentioned or understood. It had left him with a longing he could not decipher, almost sexual.

Peaks of a drunken disagreement from the quartermaster's alleyway rose from the deck below him, though he could make little of what it was about. The angry shouting began to fill his consciousness. Then, as he bent over the rail to make out more, he recognised a diversion, a trick which was not of their making.

'No.' He spoke out loud in recognition. And as he lifted his head, his attention was taken by what looked like a sail, a lateen sail, about a point on the starboard bow, reaching fast, without lights, perhaps on a collision course with the ship. For a moment the sail was silhouetted against the pale night. It came on steadily towards the ship, its course unaltering.

On the bridge there was no sign of the pipe. Radnor ran up the wheelhouse steps two at a time. Inside, there was only the quartermaster, his weary, resentful features dim in the glow from the binnacle.

'Starboard your wheel!' Radnor's voice rang through the darkness. 'Bring her round on to two four zero.'

'Two four zero sir,' the quartermaster repeated, suddenly awake. 'Two four zero it is, sir.'

'Right.' Radnor picked up the glasses and scanned the sea on the port side of the ship. 'Where the fuck's the third mate?'

'Chart room, sir.' There was something in the quartermaster's tone. Radnor went over to peer into the man's face. He was grinning.

'What is it, Murphy?'

'Nothing, sir.'

Radnor let it go and went back to the front of the bridge to resume his search. He found nothing. Whatever it was, had gone.

'See a sail again, sir?' Murphy said after a while.

It was true, earlier in the voyage Radnor had spotted a sail, or sails, off Cape St Vincent. A three-masted barque appearing briefly from a bank of mist. No one else had caught a glimpse of her. A training ship perhaps, maybe one of the Portuguese. Murphy's cynicism bothered him. He glanced up at the compass repeater on the deck head. 'Look to your course, Murphy!'

The old man came storming into the wheelhouse, followed closely by the third mate, both cannoning into Radnor who was on his way out on to the wing of the bridge.

'What the hell's going on? What the blazes are you up to, Murphy? Course recorder's drawing pretty pictures back there!'

'Dhow,' Radnor said flatly, 'no lights,' and went on outside to continue the search. The other two followed, and for several minutes they all stood searching the empty sea in all directions.

'Well, I don't know about that,' Archibald Peeke grumbled finally, his pipe flicking to every syllable, 'y'must be seeing things! Bring her back on to one seven five, Murphy, please,' he called back to the wheelhouse.

'One seven five sir . . . one seven five it is, sir.'

'Steady as she goes.'

'Steady on one seven five, sir.'

Silence.

The three men returned to searching with their binoculars all round the ship, a huge slick of phosphorescence marking her last turn like a giant question mark. Inside, Murphy was smirking into the weak light of the compass card.

Eventually Radnor said quietly, 'There was definitely a dhow out there. They must've altered under our stern.' He turned to go back inside the wheelhouse, but now there were the beginnings of doubt and uncertainty in his mind. He placed the binoculars back into the little wooden slot at the front of the wheelhouse and retired. Soon afterwards, the captain also melted away, leaving the third officer alone.

Later that evening Radnor sat in his day cabin awaiting the inevitable knock on the door from Archie Peeke, wanting his game of chess and a chat. He was trying to remember, as he sat there on his daybed, when it was he'd first recognised the conscious thought – not the germ which had always been there, but the completed, conscious thought that one day soon he might walk off the ship, for good. Leave the sea.

'Leave her to her strange biddings,' he said, the words crackling out of him. He regretted them immediately. He hardly dared think such things, let alone say them. He must say nothing. Yet this idea had already become familiar to him, if it was not already an intention. Again he checked himself, trying to bend his mind away. For he knew that, beating next to his own heart, another had begun to grow, keeping such perfect time with his own, he could not distinguish between the two. Yet he knew it was there, and as much as he wished it were not so, there could never be any secrets from this other, inside himself.

Again he saw the sails of the great three-masted barque, and the dhow. Both unseen by others, both seen by him. And always these things would happen after a kind of infidelity. That was after all what it was, when such thoughts as leaving the sea came to him.

He sprang to his feet, seeing with the sudden, dreamless clarity of a man condemned.

'May I come in?' Captain Peeke stood on the threshold. 'Are you feeling all right, Bob? You look grey.'

He was already inside Radnor's dayroom, holding in one hand his mug of gin and water, and in the other his chess set, which he bent to place on the little table with a grunt, and straightened with a snort of surrender to his own enduring lack of condition.

He faced Radnor in the thick yellow light of the cabin lamp, took a sip from his mug and pulled out his pipe from the breast pocket of his shirt before ramming it into his mouth. He sat down rather suddenly and awkwardly, and began setting out the board. 'You start then,' he said.

They sat opposite each other, heads down, saying nothing. As the game progressed, the captain took gulps from his mug, blowing out his cheeks and swallowing as he studied the board before making another ill-considered move, and Radnor, always several moves ahead, following through his scheme, with charitable boredom, his mind on other things.

'Checkmate,' Radnor said at last. It happened every night, within about half an hour. But Peeke never minded, always wanting to come back for more the next evening or the next. It was something about the physical act of playing that he found comforting. He was not really interested in the game itself.

'These pieces are pretty ropey, aren't they,' Radnor said as they packed them away. 'Why don't I carve some new ones?'

'Could you?'

'Yes. Easy enough.'

Peeke took the final draught from his mug, hissing out the vapour between his teeth as he examined his first officer.

'That dhow or whatever it was – did a disappearing act, didn't it?'

Radnor made no reply. Peeke looked down at his feet.

There was a long silence.

Peeke ventured, 'Might not have been there, of course.' He crossed his arms, leaning forward on the table. 'Not possible you imagined it?'

'No.' Radnor was emphatic. 'Not imagined, I'm afraid, Archie. It was there.'

Another long pause, Peeke turning it over in his mind.

'That barque,' he said at length, 'I reported her to Lloyds. Did you know? They came back with nothing. According to their researches, there would have been nothing of that description around there at that time.'

Radnor thought about this. 'I can only say that I saw what I saw, plain as my hand. Why should I make it up? She came out of the mist and went back into it again. I don't know what else I can say. What are you driving at?'

'Well, the trouble is, Bob, it happened to be the third officer's watch, both times. The lad's very young. Very inexperienced. It's knocked his confidence. We have to be sure of ourselves.' Peeke shook his head. 'You see, I can't understand it. I was up there all evening, apart from a couple of minutes in the chart room. And I saw nothing!'

'She had no lights, Archie. Probably smuggling.'

'Even so, on such a night.'

Peeke began lighting his pipe, the spurts of flame illuminating a woeful expression. Shaking out the match behind clouds of smoke, he said, 'No, I don't understand it.' He puffed out more smoke until the cabin was full of it, but his expression slowly changed to a smile, then to the edge of laughter. 'Except you're the only one who can see these things, Bob!'

Radnor was not prepared to surrender to this. He said nothing.

Peeke returned to the point. 'Look, this is the second time it's happened within a few days and the voyage has barely begun. And what about that other time last trip, Mozambique Channel, wasn't it? I mean, how can I put it? I know you, Bob. We've known one another a long time, haven't we? You know what I'm saying. Is it not just possible . . . ?'

'No, Archie, it is not.'

Peeke wriggled about in his seat. He gestured with his hand. 'Talk.'

Radnor nodded. He knew. Of course he knew. But he couldn't simply sit back and watch a disaster unfold. That was the alternative. They wouldn't want that, would they?

What he did understand though was that he himself might have provoked the incident. This was very different from imagining it, which was clearly what Archie suspected. What happened, happened as an exterior event. He'd even heard the shouts of the Arab seamen. Others had had similar experiences, he knew. But knowing this did not help him now, especially with this growing sense of something shadowing him. Watching, listening, all the while. He had often joked that the sea would get him in the end. Such flippancy so often comes true. But here was an inevitability, a truth gathering a mass all its own. Once that sort of thing starts there is no way of stopping it, until it is spent.

Why had he been encouraged so strangely in the first place by his old nautical school headmaster, the Reverend Fry? Why was it? What had Fry really known? He'd been a naval chaplain before taking up teaching. He'd spent half his life at sea. So oddly confiding, when he'd drawn him aside that day to tell him that he, Radnor, was a born seaman, that he could see it like words on a page. What had he seen? Of the thousands of seamen known to him, he'd said, only a handful were what he might have called 'born seamen'. He'd warned Radnor that to betray such incipient talents would be a great wrong to oneself as well as to God. Radnor had accepted all this without question, as he'd accepted most things. Now, when it was all too late, he could not understand why this had been. But Fry had always been careful to have God on his side in getting his own way, especially in administering the sudden clutches of beatings which had seemed to consume him at certain stages of every term, justifying them with an assumption of vicarious guilt. Radnor had endured it all. It had buoyed him up in a way, given him purpose, stiffening, identity.

But when he did go to sea, striking out from the shore of such certainties, he'd begun to lose his will, his belief, and finally his nerve, and each time he'd circled back in a long, slow arc to rediscover those early convictions, he'd found nothing. He felt he'd been tricked, cast out like a naked baby.

'It's coincidence, Archie,' he said, still half lost in thought. 'These sort of things happen, you know that. It's only odd because we've had two close together. Coincidence, that's all it is. But then, isn't that the way of things?'

Peeke thought about it. You couldn't live at such close quarters with someone without getting to know them pretty well. And there'd been changes in Radnor. He knew that, though what exactly, he couldn't say.

When one of the apprentices was sent down to wake him at four the next morning Radnor was so soundly asleep that

44

the boy failed to get even the smallest response. He might just as well have been dead, for all his shaking and bellowing. So they'd sent down one of the quartermasters.

The *Golden Delta* carried six white quartermasters, having their own mess deck below the officers and apprentices, but above the crew. They were not encouraged to mix with either of these groups. Somehow separate, they were normally the last to be informed of anything. Yet despite this isolation, carrying inevitable resentments, they could at least enjoy the perspective it allowed them. They viewed their chief officer with a certain amusement. This, apart from his rather prickly nature, was due to no more than his habit of muttering to himself as though he were conversing with someone invisible. Lately, he'd become something of an object of their mockery, a butt for practical jokes. On one occasion, they'd almost gone too far.

The hours soon after darkness when Radnor watched from his chair on the boat deck was the time that these men, having little to occupy themselves, would sit with their bottles, scoffing, grumbling, deriding the ship, the food, the voyage, sometimes each other – anything to temporarily obscure their own condition. They'd got it from somewhere that Radnor had some interest in the supernatural and was given to certain deeply held beliefs, though no one seemed to know exactly what these were. And so, as part of a plan, they began to stage fervent, sometimes quarrelsome discussions on their own deck just below where he sat, concerning ghosts, phantom ships, mermaids, mermen, that sort of thing. Not forgetting 'the face' that one or two of them claimed to have seen. This was a face of sorts which appeared at sea, outside portholes where no person could possibly be.

Life at sea being for some a more or less empty existence, it was Radnor's view, as he sat in his chair listening to these things, that they were attempting to thrill themselves, inviting the unknown, spooking themselves for want of anything better to do. At this he shook his head one night before returning to his cabin to continue some pencil sketches he'd been doing. One of these featured a ship very like the *Golden Delta* if not the *Golden Delta*, struggling through an impossible maelstrom, and another he'd just finished showed the same ship, almost overcome by the weight of water on her decks. These sketches were well executed in charcoal and showed not only an understanding of the medium, but a knowledge of the sea such as few artists could ever match. There were other things about the drawings both revealing and hidden. If you looked carefully into the patterns of water, there were faces and forms there. Though the harder you concentrated on these forms, the quicker they would disappear into the sea's surface. Sometimes, for a moment, the whole picture might appear to be taken up by a single entity. Yet it was impossible to hold on to it or to identify exactly what it was. They seemed to forbid scrutiny, these shapes. Radnor was always careful to hide his work. The thought of someone else ever seeing it produced an intense vulnerability in him.

As he sat there in his swelling desolation he would look up at his porthole, and on this night saw in it his own image craving the conviction he could not give. At first the change in his reflection did not penetrate his preoccupation. He saw it only as a conspiracy of light as he watched his reflection moving as he moved. But now there was something else. Something on the outside of the glass. He peered forward, leaning towards it. Whatever it was, was moving quite independently of his own reflection. He began to make out a head, with hair wet and knotted, swinging with a constant, rhythmic movement.

Radnor's deepening preoccupation was again confirmed by this incarnation. He kicked out, forcing his chair back, but in the process toppled over, the back of his head hitting the deck.

Somewhere above him, the quartermasters were convulsed in suppressed laughter. They barely had the strength between them to haul Evans, by far the simplest amongst them, back up the side of the ship. They'd persuaded him to hang suspended by a rope upside down, outside Radnor's port-hole, head bound with lengths of frayed rope, his upside-down features painted like the Cyclops, his mouth as his single eye, and his eyes and eyebrows as one huge mouth. Evans had agreed to this to gain the kudos and recognition he wanted.

'He took it . . . ! Fuck. Hook line and . . . He fell over backwards!' Evans was shaking with fright and exhilaration as they dragged him up over the rail and on to his feet. 'I think we might've gone too fuckin' far.'

They untied his trembling ankles, disposing of any evidence over the side, attending to him in a rare moment of fellowship.

'Give 'im something to think about then,' someone whispered.

They giggled like a gang of kids.

'Christ, to have seen his face!'

They wasted no time in cleaning up everything and getting below, but once there Evans persisted, 'I think we should see if he's all right. I think we went a bit fuckin' far.'

'So you keep saying. You mean *you* went a bit fucking far.'

Evans protested, his voice getting shriller, 'He went over, hit his head. He didn't move!'

As bottles of beer were being wrenched open, they said, 'Off you go then. Go and see what damage you've done!'

Goading him on, pleased with themselves as they drank determinedly, they jostled Evans out on to the deck.

★   ★   ★

47

Some while later Evans timidly pushed ajar the door to the officers' accommodation and went in. Most of the doors into the cabins were hooked back with curtains drawn across. In time to the gentle roll of the ship, these swung very slowly into the alleyway and back again, so that as he crept past Evans could see the comfortable, unfamiliar carpets inside the cabins. He stopped outside the chief officer's door and peeked through the gap at the side of the curtain. The captain sat at a table, a chessboard laid out in front of him, his pipe flicking up and down in his mouth as he spoke. Then edging along a bit further, peering in at a more oblique angle, Evans could just distinguish the mate, standing with a glass in his hand. They were like waxwork models in a museum.

By the time Evans had returned to the others, his relief at finding Radnor none the worse for his experience had already changed to vainglory.

It was coincidence that put Evans in Radnor's cabin later on the night of the dhow sighting, with the job of rousing the mate from a peculiarly deep sleep after the apprentice had failed to wake him.

Evans found Radnor sleeping quietly. Before he woke him, he went through into the dayroom, running his fingers in a dilatory way over the surfaces in an offhand violation of Radnor's privacy. The cabin was pretty bare, no photographs, books, magazines, wireless – only some clean laundry in a pile on the table. Evans was disappointed. He wanted some little trophy with which to lift himself in the eyes of his mates. But there was nothing, and such an opportunity ... He returned to Radnor. Seeing him there, Evans thought he did look somehow odd. He shook him. 'One bell, sir!' No response. Radnor's breathing did not falter. 'Sir ... Mr Radnor, your watch!' he shouted into his ear, shaking him vigorously, but Radnor remained oblivious. There was no evidence of drink. Evans quailed again when he thought of the night of their tomfoolery. He shook him again. 'Your watch now, Mr Radnor, your watch!' The violence of this last pummelling dislodged a blue sketchbook from under his pillow. Evans picked it up; it was full of sketches and notes. He flicked through it gleefully, and as he did so Radnor opened his eyes and stared at Evans, but as if he were blind and not seeing. Evans dropped the hand with the book in it to his side, obscuring it from view.

A little time went by, the two men facing each other in silence. Radnor did not appear to register anything. But when Evans began to speak, Radnor said, 'What the hell do you want, Evans?' The question stated that it wasn't customary for the quartermasters to call the officers.

'Ah, you're awake, sir – the apprentice had a spot of bother rousing you. He wondered whether you were all right.'

'I'm perfectly all right, thank you, Evans. I shall be up there in five minutes.'

Evans dropped the sketchbook into his trouser pocket as he turned to go. He hadn't intended taking the book, but there was nothing else he could do with it now. Before going back up to the bridge, he went to the quartermaster's alleyway and stuffed it behind a ventilator shaft.

'He's on his way,' he said, breezing on to the bridge.

Within minutes Radnor had arrived to take over the watch, and shortly after that another quartermaster came to relieve Evans. Radnor didn't speak, his energies directed towards his watchkeeping duties at first. He was tracing around a worn pattern which was the only life he knew. It was only later, with certain jobs out of the way, that he began to brood over his missing sketchbook.

Over the following days, it was plain Radnor suspected Evans of theft. He had searched everywhere in his cabin and later interrogated the apprentice, satisfying himself that the boy was innocent. He wasn't fond of this set of quarter-masters. He'd sailed with Murphy and Evans before. Evans was a weak man, impressionable, untrustworthy, 'a griper', the captain called him, and so he was. And Murphy – a much older man, a seaman all his life, perhaps in his early sixties and like so many, resentful of his own impotence to resist a further voyage. A troublemaker. If there was a problem, he'd probably be there, goading, often with too much alcohol inside him, with a defiant teetering grin, always seeing himself as quite blameless.

Seamen are famous for their hobbies, to fill the empty hours – model-making of one form or another, scrimshaw, collecting stamps, studying by correspondence course. These days, Radnor had begun to lose patience with it all, believing that somehow such things were an irrelevance. Nevertheless his writings and drawings showed a growing absorption with some arbitrary hand which held sway over the sea, a hand which could be upset by the smallest thing. An uncertain state of affairs, well reflected in what he wrote and drew. His fear of what might overtake him if a sense of his inten-tion (not intention even, merely the possibility of his free will operating in the matter of his own future) were suspected by this mysterious Godhead, harried him to every corner of the ship, and even planted in his mind the word, which sometimes he spoke out aloud on the point of waking, 'defection'. These liquid fears ran from his heart to be cast in the pages of his sketchbook in words and pictures. He could not, nor did he wish to, make the theft public, hoping to recover the book without attracting too much attention. Thieving on board ship has always been a serious crime, carrying with it, not so long ago, the heaviest penalties; for even now, having once made such a thing known, it will poison the small and disparate community. He would sort this thing out quietly.

Summoning one of the apprentices, he asked him to relay a message to the quartermasters. He would like to see them all on the boat deck after their smoko at say 11.15, but if he was a few minutes late, they were to wait. He knew that one of them, perhaps two, would be sleeping their watch below, but Evans on the twelve to four and Murphy on the four to eight would both be about. He also knew the ship thoroughly, and where sailors liked to hide things. A few minutes before time he slipped down to the main deck, feeling the air fresher as it funnelled past the chains, so close to the sea, the breeze picking up the light spray from the bow wave so that he felt it cool on his face and arms. In fine weather he could not resist these seductions, they lifted him out of his struggle – the closer he was to the sea herself the more rapturous he became, and wanting, wanting . . . what? He stopped to lean over the rail watching the hissing white water sucking along the wall of the hull. It was a violation, this ship, its massive propellers hollowing out the sea. It didn't live with it as a twig or branch, swinging easily with the waves, or a boat with a sail. It was opposed to it, simply. Why was it here anyway, this great ship full of boilers and machinery and oil and tractors and tyres and locomotives and pipes? What were these things that ship after ship carried to other worlds? What was all this commotion? Looking down into the clawing white and feeling for a handhold to pull himself up and on to the rail he began to lift himself off the deck, and he saw the deep blue stretch pure to the horizon and then he pushed himself with all his strength suddenly back inboard and into the path of a sailor struggling with a great number of paint tins so that they all clattered against the bulkhead, pots of paint every-where, and streams of black and white flowing together

51

through the scuppers, pumping out over the side with each roll, and glistening along the rusting hull.

'Sa'b!'

Radnor fell across the rail, watching the paint run all the way to the sea, then pushed himself upright, swivelling round quickly, apologising and hanging the pots back on the man as though he were a pack mule. The sailor submitted to this, occasionally muttering something in Hindi, an expression of deep repugnance pulling his stubbly chin back on to his neck and tightly puckering his lips, before he continued his journey aft, tripping away under his much lighter burden, the encounter suddenly forgotten. Radnor could not move; he was stunned like a bird having flown into glass and he watched the wiry little sailor, his bare feet stuffed into a pair of old trodden-down shoes and his brown legs shining with the sea spray, until he disappeared into the dark hole of the bos'n's store beneath the fo'c'sle head.

By the time he reached the quartermaster's alleyway Radnor had recovered, and quickly began checking the vacant cabins. Only two quartermasters were there, sleeping, as he'd suspected. In the mess he unscrewed all the observation hatches in the air ducting, and standing on a chair searched with a torch through the pipes. There were bundles of pornographic photographs, cartons of cigarettes, tobacco, furtive little tins sealed with elastic bands, all stashed haphazardly around the openings, but there was no book. He looked everywhere and found nothing. He even looked rather lamely for something with which he might bargain with Evans, but again nothing, so, glancing at his watch, he quickly started back to his cabin.

In one of the alleyways deep within the ship, a cream-painted rectangular tunnel of steel, he felt winded suddenly as if by a fist in his guts, and he fell against the bulkhead, actually knocking that part of the back of his head still tender from falling over in his chair the night of the hoax. It seemed to have the effect of knocking him wider awake, as though he had been partially asleep, the memory of events still there in his mind but distant, not entirely belonging to him, a span of life over which there had been inadequate control. There was fear now and panic, panic at what he might have done at the rail a little earlier, but anchored by his present purpose. And so he pressed on, catching sight he thought, when he glanced behind him, of someone who might have been watching.

To those quartermasters who waited, there seemed nothing different about him when he arrived a little late for their appointment.

He told them the captain had been concerned that the deck passengers to be picked up in Jeddah, all pilgrims returning from Mecca, should not fall victim to the horse-play he had sometimes known on previous voyages. The sort of thing he was referring to, and for which he would punish the perpetrators severely, was the game of pointing the pilgrims in the wrong direction when they asked where Mecca was in relation to the ship. Lines and lines of them all bowing to a great fetch of empty ocean, or a shanty on Socotra. It wasn't funny. 'A game perhaps,' the captain had protested, 'but a blasphemy I will not allow on my ship.' He had sat back in his chair and reflected, then, emphasising the rhythm of his words, 'To point them all in the wrong direction when they are in the middle of an ocean and find it funny.' There followed a display of melancholy where he shook his head slowly, perhaps deep in thought, but it was a posture of resignation he would often adopt and with which he felt comfortable. Picking up suddenly and right-eously, leaning forward again, 'They are to be afforded all the consideration possible under their circumstances as deck passengers, and any questions of . . . navigation, should be referred to one of the navigating officers, and no one else.'

All this, Radnor now passed on. He was still regaining his breath as he spoke to the little gang of unresponsive faces, looking at each in turn, eliciting their consideration, favour, goodwill, but getting nothing in return. They were unmoved, all of them, but they studied him, if he was not imagining it, with just a hint of amusement.

Watched by Western eyes from the upper decks, the pilgrims filed aboard at Jeddah, congregating in groups on the hatch covers, standing about in the vaporous heat, diffident, unsure of this other world, keenly aware of the desultory surveillance from above, yet finally settling down with their cloth bundles, satisfying themselves with little more than a patch of canvas for their savings – a miniature society of men falling as easily into its own patterns as a grizzled face into its own familiar expressions.

It took a morning to complete the process of embarkation and formalities before the vessel was ready for sea again, heading this time for Port Sudan. At first, life was little affected by the unfamiliar throng about the decks, but it was soon apparent that an entire shanty street was being born – small erections, makeshift shelters of dunnage appeared all over the hatch covers, the steel deck was the street itself, and the scuppers latrines, sour in the heat, and hosed through morning and evening with sea water.

Archie Peeke looked down from his high stool at the bridge windows and took a dim view of it all. Lord only knew what the owners were thinking about, cluttering up the ship in this manner, but what could he do? He didn't like to see these huts and things, littering the place; it would be dangerous if the weather turned. One sea taken green over the bows and that would be that, and all that flying debris. It didn't bear thinking about. But it was shelter for the poor beggars, he supposed. He would have a word with Radnor, over chess. Radnor. The captain turned away from the windows and looked down. He couldn't afford to lose his first officer. His general anxiety surfaced with a specific thought. The two of them had, from time to time, as might be expected, touched on matters unearthly, or rather Radnor had done so, expediently Peeke had always thought, perhaps to establish boundaries which, it must be said, remained only a short way beyond a mere knowledge of the other's physical presence. An unwavering agnostic, Peeke believed he could smell a religious man at a hundred paces, and Radnor was certainly not one of those. But these days, these days, he'd begun to wonder. It seemed odd to think it, but there was a sort of flavour about him now, without doubt. What was it? Every look, every gesture, betrayed it. A mute potential for preachiness. 'I don't know,' he blurted out, running his hand over his mouth and turning back towards the windows, and those pilgrims. Well, it was possible after all. In the end, he thought, you can become so tired there is only faith or suicide left. He hardly speaks now, except when it is absolutely necessary, and when he does . . . He glanced over to the third mate, who seemed lost, gazing down at the precarious cluster of hovels and tents, and the growing number of people now squatting on their prayer mats and doing obeisance towards a place directly astern of the ship, making it look, or so Peeke allowed himself briefly to imagine, as though it might be the bewildered young third mate they were venerating.

'I'm not so sure that our passengers may not have rather overdone their temporary accommodation,' he said later to Radnor. 'I know they have to have somewhere, but I've never seen anything quite like this lot. I'm uneasy. I suggest it wouldn't be a bad idea if we "tidy" 'em up a little, don't you think? I don't like to see it.'

Radnor made no reply to this, remaining glum, staring at the deck, elbows on knees, hands nursing a bottle of beer.

Eventually Peeke objected, 'Look Bob, for God's sake . . .'

'I was thinking,' he retorted, but still completely absorbed and making no movement whatsoever, and then again with a kind of brooding challenge, 'thinking'.

'Well, something ought to be done.' Peeke fidgeted, his words carrying their meaning home so that Radnor glanced up quickly. As he spoke, Peeke too was brought up short by the recognition that he could no longer bury his head over this matter of his first officer, things could not be allowed to slide any further. He really had no alternative now but to have it out once and for all, to find out exactly what it was that seemed to be eating him up so. But that is precisely what he did not do when, ignoring everything and compensating with limp unconcern and more than his usual measure of gloominess, he said, 'I think we'll have to have 'em down, don't you? All of 'em.'

Radnor had once again been brooding over his sketchbook, wondering whether to bring it up with Archie. Perhaps he had already seen it, this little book which would reveal the nature of his fear and belief, or unbelief. How many eyes had now seen it, he wondered. 'I was going to ask . . .' His voice was hoarse, the words broken as if by some obstinate bubble in his throat, blowing itself up, throttling him. The captain, momentarily taken aback then filling again with an attitude of responsible unease as though he might have expected this sort of thing, rose and landed a hefty blow once, twice across Radnor's shoulders, and then as promptly returned to his seat, leaving Radnor, still waving him away, to cough violently, his face a deep plum colour, draining quickly pale and troubled. 'Ah God . . .' he said, 'I'm sorry.' Swallowing and coughing again more freely, the captain watching, anxiously. But just then something appeared to take Radnor's attention; this he seemed to resist for a while. It was the antidote to his fit yet somehow kindred to it. The captain was on the point of asking what it was when Radnor abruptly swivelled round. 'Did you hear that . . . see . . . ?' He didn't wait for a reaction, but shot across to his desk, clumsily half climbing on to it, upsetting a box of wood chips and shavings as he went, and some rudely carved chess pieces – all rolling on to the deck. Peering up into the night through his half-open porthole, he craned his head this way and that and then clambered up higher on to his desk to get a better view downwards along the hull, both ways, and into the sea churning past in the dim light of the portholes. There was the sort of quickening urgency about him that a dog exhibits, pressing its face against the wires of a cage to get a last glimpse of its departing mistress. Then he looked out over the calm sea with its reflections of the night, felt it draw him so that his surroundings began to fade as before and he forced himself away from there and the open sea breeze, stumbling back, having seen nothing.

All the while Captain Peeke sat quietly, watching, collected and removed from this latest outbreak, until finally Radnor returned, humiliated again by yet another exhibition. It had come at the wrong moment, that's all, this nightly or almost nightly visit. But that it had done so at all despite another's presence seemed to strengthen its reality for Radnor.

'You were saying,' the captain went on as if nothing had filled the space between.

'You saw nothing?' Radnor's question stated, his voice resigned, almost self-reproachful. He picked up his beer and drained it in one, starting to cough again as he put the bottle back on the table, soon recovering but withdrawing again into himself. He would have to submit now. He would have to systematically reveal everything, lay out the whole unrecognisable jigsaw. Nothing was indeed secret or permitted to be.

It was vanity to hide, yet hiding was the only safe place. Always harnessed! Always shackled! This inexplicable union, furthering what? It was there, Radnor thought, all there, on the face of that poor man the night they hanged him in Carthage, the ship's company, orderly, in ranks, waiting, the sense of vengeance, outrage, deepening. Yet so thrown were they all by the act itself, momentous yet insignificant, that for a moment everything was changed, and the captives and their masters stirred in one instant together, standing figures whose long shadows merged in the dust, completing one single pattern, the only movement the execution itself.

How could he begin to explain? He wanted more air than he could breathe. Then there was a moment when he thought he could tell the whole story and he started out, 'I heard . . .' He laughed. 'Well, I thought I heard . . . recently, sometimes I've heard something, I'm not sure.' He stopped. And instead, finding the spirit to 'go on' in name only, he lied with frank, intimate, defeat. 'I'm tired, Archie, that's all, dog-tired. I caught flu in London. Haven't felt myself since.'

For Captain Peeke, unable to face what he feared, this was a satisfactory expedience. Of course, it didn't explain things, but it was something. 'Bob,' he said, leaning forward, confiding. 'I've been thinking. Look, I know we've got our work cut out for the one day at Port Sudan, but there's nothing there that I and the second can't handle. You get ashore and stretch your legs, you're no good to us in your coffin!' Beaming, he picked up his pipe and lit it, his satisfaction illuminated at each spurt of flame until he shook the match out and flicked it triumphantly, still smoking, through the half-open port, then leant back and crossed his legs. 'Well I mean to say, stay aboard of course if you want, I know Port Sudan doesn't exactly offer the best . . . but, you know, do what you want. Have a break from the ship, a complete break from the ship. I'm going to stand your watch for a while until you've shaken this thing off. I can see now, this heat. Nothing like a rest. You'll be as right as rain in a few days.'

Of course Peeke was not being quite straight with him, but quite apart from that, it was precisely what Radnor could not face. Work was a function of defence, and he acquiesced only after strongly objecting.

When Archie Peeke left a little while later, he emphasised from the safety of the other side of the door before he closed it that from now on he would be dealing with the pilgrim business himself; 'and if you ask me', he said, 'you should take my advice and grab the opportunity for a complete rest.' Then the door closed, Peeke's words hanging in the air. Radnor was left to the vacuum, to his doubt and his fear, finally falling to think about what they might have talked about: how after walking up the main deck he'd been struck, as he always had been out East, by the ingenuity of these people, how nothing, absolutely nothing was wasted and how they used things cast off by the Western crew, to clever, original, sometimes beautiful, not to say practical effect. Even though their shelters were perhaps a hazard on the foredeck of a tramp steamer they were fine examples of the barefoot skills Radnor so much admired. The timeless engineering in some of those little hutches, the ingenious joints they used, intrigued him in the same way as he'd been fascinated by the way dhows were built, unchanged for centuries, like the little Norwegian ourselver boat, built in much the same manner today as it had been a thousand years ago. Surely, he thought, these kinds of biding, innocent skills might be absorbed respectfully into the modern world? Certainly he himself felt comforted by them, even supported. Yet the nature of this precariousness, the allure of shinier things, was plain. Walking up the deck towards the fo'c'sle head he'd watched them beating out discarded tins into fine teapots and cooking utensils, making them into small stoves and plates, and he'd wanted to say how he'd felt ashamed suddenly, ashamed of this great ship with its voracity and belching waste, and then there had been the little wood carvings offered for sale, painstakingly done, with here and there the kind of pressed tin jewellery, photograph holders and the like found in the cheapest shops at home, but it was these things, he'd noticed, that were peddled with the most thrill. He'd wanted to talk about all this.

For some long while after the captain had gone Radnor did not move. He seemed abandoned, his eyes dead, fixed on the door just closed. A flicker of life passed across his features, a momentary brightening, when he might have moved, changed, gone with the time, but in that instant he switched back to the door and so but for the unbroken hum of the engine, and the faint hiss of sea on the breeze, a noise so familiar it was like silence, in that time there were no other sounds. He sat there quite still and at last began to inflate the notion that Archie must have known all along: that it was not simply a matter of fatigue, or flu. As time passed the conviction grew. He had been relieved of his appointment, that was what had happened, deftly and without fuss, relieved of his duties, but temporarily, temporarily, until that is, perhaps . . . The spell was broken now; he shuffled about in his chair, stood up, turned, looking out across the sea.

That night Radnor slept fitfully, always waking from a ferment of little nightmares into his darkening fear. Many of these snapshots of barbarity he had actually witnessed, but they grew now, distorted from the actual events. Appalling as they undoubtedly had been in reality, they held a deeper, even more chilling property in sleep. But more than this, on the edge of consciousness he found he knew something of unresolvable truths, which melted away as soon as he tried to hold them in his mind, remembering nothing more when he awoke than something intimate, and as familiar as passing his hand over parts of his own body.

There was one dream which recurred and was a prelude to such insights. He and thousands of others waited in a line snaking over plains of hard mud, where the Ganges delta had, all but the main channels, dried up. They stood, orderly, unquestioning, all life gone out of them, in this serpentine order, and slowly inch by inch, dream by dream, shuffled forward towards a primitive wooden structure of ropes and poles and planks, where somewhere unseen a man, a solitary man, wrapped up in a pure white robe with a hood and splattered with blood, was calling the next one to the platform. Here each one lay, innocent, to be carved alive in a great silence of open sky, the dark blood beginning to refill the empty rivulets that ran towards the central course. He felt the instinct for blood and sacrifice, the timeless cycle: the sudden unexplained whirlwind and the vain clear calm. The more he turned his head away, the more vividly he saw. He awoke, feeling a sphere small in his palm, a dense ball, heavier and more concentrated than anything he could imagine, and yet almost unable to confine it within his own outstretched arms it was so open and ethereal, and this one whole familiar sensation having itself a name, a word, which he could not possibly know.

Finally, late on in the night, the dreaming ended and he was left alone with his knowledge and a dark paralysis, unable, however he tried, to move a muscle. He could not guess how long he remained in this black insentient cocoon until at last, mercifully, he felt his limbs again and opened his eyes. He rolled over to look at the clock on the bulkhead. It was fifteen minutes to four, the time he was normally called for his watch.

Then remembering the previous evening and all that it held, the captain, and again that light, as if it had been swung past his scuttle, but travelling so fast he could not be sure whether it was close to the ship or far off, he lay still, with a sense of weightlessness. No one knocked. As the minutes passed, he longed for the old routine to return, but five to four came, then four, and nothing. At five past he was still in his bunk. The ship was rolling more now. He heaved himself into a sitting position, his head resting against the bulkhead, and turning it to one side felt the bruise and still the sharp jabbing pain, and through the open porthole heard sounds of the sea and a stronger, much stronger sense of it. He had condemned himself with his own defence, he thought. His own talents were growing deeper, but more susceptible by the day, in a way which seemed to oppose the uses to which they had always been put.

He dressed and went out on to the boat deck, pacing back and forth across the full width of the ship, feeling the closeness of land and changes in soundings but seeing only the lights of ships astern moving north towards Suez, nothing ahead, only a faint smell of dusty earth on the wind. The bridge was dark, no sign of life, the funnel wiping its vapour across the stars, melting them for a moment in the arc of the ship's roll, and beneath his feet the deck snowy in the night light. He moved soundlessly to one rail, running his eyes briefly over the swell, and then to the other. At each turn he hesitated, hand on the rail, looking down into the ocean, the ship's downward roll taking him past the point where something of his own self-governance was left behind and so, gripping the rail, he swung down with the sea, its white phlegm streaming past, a giddying fairground loop in silent uproar, until the roll hauled him back and into his old trade, his habit drawing his eyes up, vigilant again and about the horizon. And so it went on for an hour or so, back and forth, without a spell. Then, behind the funnel, in the centre of the ship, he stopped, as if struck in sudden recognition. His attention directed behind him, he was overcome yet again by his old feeling of being shadowed. Turning slowly, he saw something which remarkably for Radnor he had not noticed till then, the dark articulations of the African coast barely recognisable to the westward. But this was not what drew his attention – there in a cleft of land about two points off the bow was the sure outline of the dhow, crossing ahead. A baggala, he thought. He moved quickly towards the rail, stopping after a few paces, staring at the dagger-shaped vessel, unlit under her lateen sail, moving cleanly. He formed a word but it went unspoken. The strengthening breeze booming into his mouth, he glanced up to the bridge, made a move towards it and stopped. Surely the little dhow had seen them, but she bore on towards the unwavering course of the *Golden Delta*. Again Radnor made towards the bridge steps and faltered, turning again, peering across the sea, noting the unchanging bearing. There was little time now. His hesitant progress towards the bridge persisted though he checked himself all the while. He thought of the passengers, turned back towards the dhow, and watched helpless as she slipped out of the cleft and disappeared before the dark of the land. Running to the rail, he gauged her speed through the darkness, timing her emergence. There was a lightening of the sky, barely perceptible, an area of sea without land or land further off, lower on the horizon, and he held his breath while the dhow sailed through the tunnel of night towards the area of feeble light. He waited, but the moment when she would have appeared passed. He prayed, beseeching it to reinvent itself, urging the little baggala out into the open water again, but still it did not show. And then, with a sudden descent into fury, he charged it to declare itself by colliding with the ship, cursing that familiar ever-sensed awareness which held him and which he dreaded so much to abandon with its undying whisper tugging, always tugging, but receding now with the lift of the land. He yelled into the blackness, his voice dizzying and trailing away as he hung down over the rail, afraid to open his eyes, unseeing of Archie Peeke observing now from the chart room. And at last he turned his back on the sea, lifting his head towards the stars, and longed for the scented earth, feeling that tension between release and loss he always suffered when closing the coast, sensing the ocean draw back, and thinking of the surf as it sucks at the stones along the shore.

It was the abrupt change in motion which finally woke Radnor. The ship heeled, by degrees, an ungainly movement, turning in calm water; this was accompanied by a change in the familiar note of the engines, which brought back an awareness of them, jolts, shudders, the ship kicking astern, manoeuvring, all culminating in the rebuttal from the stone dock as she came alongside.

Radnor struggled to his feet. Already he felt shrouded in nostalgia for the open ocean he'd so recently longed to leave. But more than that, he now suffered a kind of uneasy displacement, a dissonance, where nothing seemed to fit. It was the first time he'd entered port lying in his bunk, and at this moment he regretted the forfeiture of his trade which he should have been following on the fo'c'sle head. Instead, standing in this strangely thicker, richer sunlight, investing heavier tones in his drab cabin than the blades of sea light, his head reeled with the sudden stillness.

A little while later, on deck in the rising heat, he saw the pilgrims retreat to the shade of their hovels, defensive, watchful, drawing in what little they had around them, while stevedores, their thick hair decorated with bleached bones, appeared oddly exuberant as they passed the cargo from hand to hand. But picking his way towards the saloon for breakfast, looking over the dusty quayside to the shunting of railway wagons, his eye level with shimmering warehouse roofs, then back to the agitated clamour of the ship, he sensed it was a certain restraint in their actions which overflowed into the outbursts of hooting, the dance going on, but the dancers always, he thought, conscious of being observed. There was a sense of habitual reference, of looking over shoulders for approval; the frantic busy fingers and darting faces – a terrorised, artificial, unseemly fervour for the business at hand.

Mealtimes in the officers' quarters were pretty much silent affairs – muttered greetings and muted, cryptic exchanges taking the place of real conversation, and always the clatter of cutlery to emphasise its absence, though on this occasion the sounds of cargo being handled, the ringing din from the scorching decks and those strange whooping cries would have discouraged all but the most determined of talkers. There was only one other person in the dining room when Radnor arrived, the deck apprentice who'd failed to wake him and who now shrank back, dropping his gaze, intent on bolting his food, caught between flight and hunger, and slipping out a minute or so later, sliding respectfully past the incoming figure of the captain.

Peeke came in and sat down in his normal position at the head of the main table next to Radnor, barely an acknowledgement between them, the sun reflecting off the starched linen cloth, throwing up such a fierce light under the chins of the two men that certain features were caught in a relative shade, producing in them a haggard look. Taking his time, Peeke tucked his napkin high around his neck, as was his custom, poking out his chin and looking upwards in patient, weighty deliberation. Raising his voice against the racket outside, he said, 'I'm off to see the agents after

breakfast. We should be ready to sail by evening. With luck!'
Then as an afterthought, 'You feeling rested?'

Radnor waited while a steward placed two enormous
plates of breakfast grill before them. He waved his away.

'You haven't lost your appetite as well, Bob?' Peeke was
already beginning to tuck in. He did not look up, more
absorbed with eating than a reply.

Radnor watched as mouthful after mouthful was shov-
elled in. Then, choosing his moment, 'I'm fine Archie, thank
you.' He was on the point of saying something else but
thought better of it and picked up a salt cellar, turning it
around in his hand, contemplating it, finally saying, 'I'm
feeling very much better. And I don't want to burden others
with my job.'

Peeke stopped, gently putting down his knife and fork,
and wiped his bulging mouth, pulling his napkin adrift and
himself dolefully back to the present. The two little knots
of muscle on either side of his mouth pulled all his features
downwards. He was unshaven after standing Radnor's watch
for him, and perspiring heavily. His jaw slowed, the last shreds
of comfort disappeared down his throat as he was cornered
by his own command, brought face to face with his dread
of isolation and the appeal to no one. This had, after all,
been the reason why he'd asked for Radnor as mate. Radnor
with that curiously brilliant intuition of his – legendary
among the deck officers of the company. For Archie, it had
always been wonderfully consoling to have him around. Until
recently. Now he felt he was being forced into a corner over
him. That extraordinary intuition seemed to have become
impaired, perverted, perhaps even threatening Radnor's
sanity. It had occurred to him earlier to wire head office
about it. But he hadn't, for Radnor's sake, and of course
hoping things would get better. Behind it all, he knew he
relied too heavily on Radnor, and it occurred to him only

now that this was probably to mask his own inadequacies as a captain. The only thing to be done at the moment, he thought, was nothing. There must be no rash or hasty move. Hope for the best. That was it. That's all he could do for now.

'Well,' he said eventually, 'it's up to you. But I feel you should have a break to get yourself properly fit. There's no great problem for a little while.'

Their eyes met, and in that vacuum who knows what crossed between them, though both in their own way wished to perpetuate the illusion that there was nothing wrong.

'Perhaps I will take the opportunity of popping ashore here as you suggested.'

'Good. That's good.' Archie smiled, returning to his breakfast, eating now with even more gusto, though hunted by fear revived by his own uncertainty.

Radnor broke off pieces of dry toast, chewing them unenthusiastically as Archie, having completed his meal, sat back swallowing belches, his face red and wet, forcing his chin down so that it doubled against his chest. At the same moment three senior engineers came in, including the chief, Angus McIver, who sat down at the head of another table next to the captain. The usual nodding acknowledgements but nothing spoken, the newcomers getting down straight away to the business of breakfast. Suddenly Peeke dumped his napkin on to his empty plate and stood up to go, then as if caught by a thought he leant over to speak in Radnor's ear. 'Seventeen hundred, we sail.' Radnor nodded and Archie then repeated himself but much louder to the chief. 'Seventeen hundred, chief – we sail!'

The chief looked up. 'You would like to sail,' he corrected.

'I would like to sail,' Peeke assented with a grin.

As Peeke stood, the chief beckoned him over.

A period passed when the shouts and jibes from the deck, the hum of the generators, the intent of the breakfasting engineers and the sun slanting through in beams of dust, all deepened for Radnor his inertia, his sense of having no bearing, no place in the world, nothing as it were to steady himself with. And beyond the ship's metal walls, always the pull, the endless sea, the clawing, frantic, struggle, the babble, mute or audible. He turned in his chair and caught the chief and Archie, both for an instant scrutinising him, but it was enough. In that fragment: their heads huddled together and Radnor's doubt hardening. He rose in the same move, and went out.

Now he had to get off the ship, so he began walking fast towards his cabin. Outside in the buffeting heat he swung round on to the stairway leading up to the boat deck. At the top, stepping back to allow him through, were Evans and Murphy. As he drew level with them they both chanted 'Morning sir', their tone mocking, contemptuous. For a moment Radnor felt goaded enough to tackle them about his sketchbook, but he only mumbled a thin response and pressed on across the deck, feeling their eyes remaining on his back. Eventually, he thought, there will come a point in any voyage when, amongst some, the common practices of everyday life, of normal conduct and cooperation, will wear thin, like the austere emergence of rocks as the tide falls, where once they were merely suspected.

Taking his rolled black umbrella for the sun, he descended the gangway on to the firm ground. Even with the ship stationary in her berth the firmness of the land was a shock, as if articulating the unease he always felt with the shore. Immediately, he longed for the ocean, those places he could recognise, so familiar to his senses. But out there where he might have lived happily anaesthetised, he had learnt he could not. He believed his penetrating instincts as a seaman had been offered to him at a price, one which deep inside himself he knew he had never paid, nor could pay. Guilt hung like smoke in his thoughts. This price, improbable, absurd though it might once have seemed, meant entering into some kind of covenant, he sensed. He could not imagine how or where or when, but knew only it had to involve a commitment he could not make. So now, having glimpsed things he was perhaps not meant to, he knew he had become a curiosity not only to his shipmates but, he understood, to the Sea herself, unveiled as he now felt himself utterly to be, always discernible, watched wherever he was.

For the moment however, he was ashore, and he walked stiffly, swinging his umbrella, fiercely deflecting the glances of dockers, parrying their natural inquisitiveness by marching unswervingly towards them if they stood in his path, so that an almost regal funnel was opened as they backed off, he with such evident purpose, they with cries of mocking, childish excitement, celebrating his passing.

But once away from them he slowed his pace along the backs of the warehouses, feeling his deep solitude but going where he knew he must.

The taxi man spotted him at once as he left the docks and, cruising the old car slowly in the dust alongside him, swung open the rear door, leant over the seat and offered his services. After haggling a price, Radnor slid in, yanking the door shut. The man spoke in Arabic, a few words, a question, but Radnor made no attempt at conversation, sitting back and looking about as the car eased over the lumpy road and into the fevered life of the town, leaving behind the masts and funnels and the high sea beyond. For a while they seemed to drive around going nowhere, the taxi driver occasionally speaking, watching Radnor in his mirror, slowing almost to a stop sometimes and driving on at a walking pace through crowds of people. The driver was enjoying himself. He grinned, hanging his arm out of the window. He seemed to know everyone, taking their hands in his as they passed. He was in no hurry and Radnor did not seem to mind. Perhaps he spoke of his passenger, showing him off as a kind of exhibit, for sometimes a small crowd would form, peering through the back windows with toothless grins, hands cupped against the glass.

As they rocked gently on through the town, Radnor found it hard to keep his eyes open, and beginning fitfully to doze, he found himself once more visiting the geometrical certainties of his youth. Then all at once he seemed to be defying his present life, holding fast, stubbornly, to the worn seat as though preventing himself from falling. He was aware, as if he was viewing everything through a bee's wing, of passing buildings, solid, mercantile, and mean low dwellings. And then the car was moving faster; an emptiness, and the perpendicular forms of people, dark exclamations against the pale earth, evenly moving, stopping to contemplate the passing car, their progress against the land imperceptible.

He was sinking into a deeper sleep as the car trundled into the little township, but when the engine cut out, the stillness and silence drew him back. He opened his eyes. The driver had already swivelled round in his seat and was eyeing him as though from some previous satisfaction. His expression said: This is the place.

There were more people gathering around now as the door was swung open and Radnor found himself looking into a cluster of faces, five or six young women, all chattering excitedly in high voices. He rolled out to stand on the hot ground, the heavy scent from a certain energy coming away from the place like steam off a boiler and it brought him up short, the void filled with a crescendo of appeals from the women who were now joined by others like a shoal of fish diverting for food. They scratched at his clothes, trying unsuccessfully to cross his gaze, but he seemed distant, stupefied. The taxi man, grinning, slumped through the open window with both arms hanging out of the car, shouted out, pawing his palm in a request for payment, everything falling quiet and the women squeezing closer to get a better look at the money. But Radnor only pointed to his watch and the driver, slow to understand, consulted his, sucking in through his teeth and blowing out with a whistle. Then at last and quite suddenly he was happy, and he began to cackle, tossing his head back, throwing his arms about before announcing satisfied, 'OK! OK!' Confirming again the time he should return by pointing to the hour, he started the engine, shoved it into gear and was gone, the dust billowing up and settling.

As the air cleared, the women once again turned their attention towards Radnor, screeching at him, pulling, vying, pandering, pushing. But he had already made his choice. She was there, circling further out, having already caught his eye, the last to arrive, and he stretched across to her over the heads of the others, the assembly swinging round in one movement, as though at the point of collective betrayal by one of their own.

Now defeated, their interest turned immediately to chagrin and scorn. Had it not been for the transcendent laughter of the girl, Radnor would have sunk deeper into the shame that this general scorn called up. But in seeing all this, the girl understood, appearing to know him, granting him peace to hide, and she led him into the cool shadows of her little hut, closing the door, firmly, gently, securely against the glare.

★   ★   ★

In the hours before the ship sailed from Port Sudan and for some time afterwards, there were auguries, so Radnor felt, like faint turbulences in the still water: returning to the ship after his run ashore, he was hardly surprised at what he found, though he stopped briefly to witness it. It was simply an expression of what he had already felt standing on deck that morning. A brawl had broken out near the special cargo locker. Rancour had flared at the first glint of contention between two Sudanese cargo handlers, swelling rapidly into ferocious conflict – lust for blood among the bystanders who quickly surrounded them, erupting with it. But then, looking through the heat to the watching figures in their fiery shapes, the clouds of dense black, smoky hair with, in its common movement, the implications of shock and impact beyond; and above it all, the baying and rallying shouts, begetting a widening orbit of attention, he no longer seemed to see, or wanted to, resuming his climb to deck level and finding Murphy, draped over the bulwark at gangway duty, joking with Evans, enjoying the fun.

'Fuckin' savages, eh?'

Condemning though he was, he grinned, enthralled by this spilling over of brutality and was held there, in the expectation of more.

Radnor paused at the quartermaster's elbow. The fighting was mostly obscured now as many of the pilgrims joined the onlookers.

'They're frightened,' Radnor said under his breath.

Murphy picked it up, spinning around.

'Frightened! You must be joking, chief!' Radnor smelt the alcohol on his breath.

Murphy turned back towards the fight, then pulled himself back again to face Radnor, tempering his manner. 'I mean . . . would you fuckin' look at 'em. Savages.' Back he turned again, unable to take his eyes off the mass of spectators now

72

forming, until . . . Radnor's words finally broke the distracted crust of his thoughts and he returned, slower this time, to his chief officer's gaze, the two men considering each other squarely. 'What would they be frightened of, sir?'

Radnor could not answer this, though his consideration of Murphy did not waver. Catching hold of the wrong idea, Murphy said, 'The pilgrims! They're scared. Yeah, yeah, dare say they are . . .' His stubbly features stretched into a grin, exposing his tiny nicotine-blackened teeth.

As they stood there, a contingent of port police came hustling up the gangway, bursting on to the main deck and running through the bystanders like a current of acid. In silence the way was opened before them, in silence it was closed behind them, everyone shuffling forward, sucked closer to the action, Murphy and Evans among them, moving stealthily at first, then with more assurance, presuming to extend the scope of their gangway duties or to forget them altogether, and chancing reproval from their chief officer which, when it came, seemed all the more shocking for being expected.

'Murphy! Evans!' Radnor's bark landed like a hail of pebbles on their backs.

Later, from the vantage of the boat deck, Radnor could see that the crisis – or this particular expression of it – had already passed, and he was struck again by the nervous, inquisitive dance of the stevedores, timidly advancing and retreating, as one of the fighters was frog-marched off the ship, and the other, trussed and bloody, was carried along behind – the police appearing to have closed the matter. And as they left the deck, ordering the resumption of work, brandishing their long batons, the other dockers followed them, seeing them to the gangway, shy, hungry, always an adroit step out of range.

By the time Radnor had grasped the handle on the door

of the officers' accommodation the two men were being thrust into the back of a waiting van. Still watching from his vantage point, Radnor felt that insinuating ache once again, his flagging sympathy for the business of the ship. He turned away from the dockside, kicking open the door into the peace and gloom of the accommodation, trying not to imagine where they would be taken to, or what might happen when they got there. Now as he entered the sanctuary of his cabin, he merely wished for some other time, washing his hands of it all, literally, and refusing to acknowledge the lengthening cast of a shadow in his head.

A little while later, after the ship had sailed, as hatches were secured and derricks lowered, a calamity occurred which brought to the surface a feeling Radnor had long borne, deeply buried. He was leaning against a rail loosely supervising the operations, watching the coast recede and the sun dropping towards the Nubian desert, diffusing into ominous spears obscured behind a shroud of dust. He rested one foot on a lower bar of the rail, his elbows on the top, hands clasped. In that moment he felt relaxed. The speed of the ship generated a welcome breeze, and all the time the coast subsided. Radnor saw the slowing movements of the crew nearing the end of their day, felt the first slight lift of the ship reaching out into deeper water, and rested his mind with Khadeja the girl, wondering what she could possibly be thinking now, she, with whom he had spent the greater part of the day in her hut, amongst her simple things, he, the butt of her calm, amused perception – his diffidence, confusion before her dignity, the shame it brought which she had seen, and somehow healed.

And now, the wake turned again among hidden reefs. A few pilgrims drifted over to the empty hatch covers to stretch out, the crew sauntered aft in the promise of a calm evening.

In this moment, hollowed by what had not yet happened, Radnor returned to earlier years, when, secure in all he knew, he had stood, in the same manner, at the same part of another ship, at the same time of day, on a similar evening. On a voyage, where? The memory was both good and bad, but strong though the echo was, he ignored its darker side, allowing it to sedate him, and stole for himself its momentary pleasure. He did not move, his skin golden in the warmth of the dying sun, his eyes almost closed. Some crewmen started up the steps leading on to the poop; he hardly saw them in these cavernous seconds. The ensign was being taken in. Then, as he turned his head to check the flag halyards, something passed downwards across his vision, dark, and slow, casting a shadow over the sun, and he cowered, instinctively, covering his head, the eyes of the falling man momentarily meeting his, as if he had already achieved a point of greater perspective and was watching Radnor rather than the other way about, the body then bouncing on the edge of a hatch directly below, for a second the skin splitting like crazy paving over the man's back.

Radnor shot a glance to the masthead, then forward along the deck to the faces of the crew all turned towards him, *him*, and in that instant, framed for always – his own position, hands over his head, and in some way culpable, as though he were a part of what had happened. He felt their eyes on him, then between him and the sailor who had fallen from the mast. They were all running along the deck then, released from the shock, and perhaps from some revelation. And he Radnor, flying down the ladders to help, and to somehow . . . exonerate himself.

They stood aside for him when he arrived, but did not, as he might have expected, return their attention to the victim; instead they remained staring at him as he passed through them . . . disconcerted, mystified, he, kneeling down beside the dead man. The crowd jostled as he went through the ritual of searching for a pulse. Of course it was only a formality. Nothing about the man lived. Radnor shook his head, and felt them press inwards on him. Standing up slowly, waving them back, he saw that half the deck passengers were there craning to get a better look.

'Stand back please!' No one moved. 'Come on!' He had to push them away, push them bodily. They backed off, sluggishly, allowing him through, but never once taking their eyes off him.

'What's up, chief!' Murphy swung into view from nowhere. 'Sewing job?'

'Find Evans and get this man up to the surgery.'

Murphy caught sight of the dead man, and froze.

'*Jildi! Jildi!*' Radnor clapped his hands. 'Get some others down here! And pass the word for the captain.'

Murphy hopped excitedly away up the deck ladders. Radnor returned to the body – a great deal of blood now. The sailors jostled each other aside to get a closer look, there was a mute appeal to Radnor, and then the long silence was broken, and everyone began jabbering at once over the body, and to him, altogether seeking something from him he could not give. He raised his hands, patting the air with his palms in a gesture both to keep them back and to crave forbearance. But as mayhem spread – some holding their heads, anguished cries of supplication, invocation, the whole deck awash with people scuttling from one place to the next and constantly to the body for repeated confirmation – Radnor noticed the sun, in all this, the sun, and the vast halo it made high over those strange violet spears stretching out for miles above the land, the sun, changed to a livid bruise, running down and across the water, and before it a watermilk smear.

With Evans back again, Radnor dimly recognised, trailing

away on to the boat deck, a string of engineers in oily boiler suits, absorbed yet removed, and a cabin steward or two, and others behind. He looked up at them from the mêlée; they watched as the dead man was rolled on to the stretcher, Murphy and Evans doubling smartly away like a couple of naval ratings with a prize, to argue about the bag, the weighting of it, and the reward. He looked up to the faces of the Europeans again, now ranged along the rail above, and felt their scorn, while all around the waiting crew looked to him. But slowly the minutes and hours left the incident behind, the event already fading with the stains on the hot canvas.

And so for two days the *Golden Delta* steamed onwards, taking a south-easterly course, breaking out of the Red Sea through the narrow Straits of Bab al Mandab into the wider waters of the Gulf of Aden and finally heading out into the Arabian Sea. Dipping rhythmically into the deep indigo, her black sides more rust streaked, her name at the stern begrimed, but her wake, a tight leash, strict in the execution of orders, describing in its straightness that hollow primacy Radnor was learning to despise – the obduracy, pride, so frightening in its blindness, and therefore the ship so . . . conspicuous that even the details of his daily round, its commonplaces, the many distractions, would not protect him from his fears. Could it really be that these fears, their mass, had become so great that they themselves attracted misfortune? They had lost three men so far, and now faced the prospect of severe weather. The events of the last hours seemed so much like totems to him. Mischance attracts attention, as a wounded fish will. But he hardly dared begin such thoughts, let alone complete them, for true as he knew them to be, it would only make them truer, more imminent, bring them somehow closer. Nothing now seemed capable of keeping such unholy ideas at bay – nothing. Except perhaps his carving of Archie's chess pieces. In this he found solace, restoring a childlike purity he had long since surrendered.

The sky continued to augur a change in the weather, the nights darker over the ocean's satin surface.

Radnor had never felt so close to the sea as now, so in tune, so uneasy. He paced through the wheelhouse on to the bridge wings, back and forth, hour after hour, the quartermaster, Murphy, at the wheel, his features lit by the dim yellow beam from the binnacle. And Murphy in his turn could see the pale, featureless lozenge which was the mate's face, passing in the darkness. Sometimes Radnor would pause outside, leaning out over the navigation lights shining their vaporous greens or reds into the night, and peer to windward in their glow, his hair matted by the strong, dank breeze. One night, in this thicker darkness, he wondered at the new weight of atmosphere, its unusual saltiness, so much stickier, fishier, as though now, sightless, they were entering an oceanic sepulchre, the whole life of the sea rising in the steamy air, to fall from time to time in dollops of warm rain, splashing on to the deck, beginning something, but coming to nothing. Radnor did not like it, his unease sharpening his senses. He leant forward over the windbreak, listening, watching. Thin blasts of air came whistling at the ship, charging and falling away. He felt Murphy's amusement at his back and said nothing.

At some time during the watch Archie Peeke appeared.

'Coastal current's giving us quite a lift,' he said, having consulted the chart and the morning fix.

Peeke could not define his concern, and they remained silent, the two of them, looking ahead. Two forms a little darker than the darkness itself.

Radnor said, 'We may find we'll have to reduce speed at some point.' But he was voicing his thoughts, ahead of the present.

There was a movement from the binnacle and a sound like a stifled sneeze. Peeke protested, 'Reduce speed! What are you talking about?' He slid away, draping himself over the windbreak on the port side, searching ahead.

Radnor remained where he was, also peering into the darkness.

A full ten minutes passed before, quite expected in these busy waters, against the faint illumination of a thinning cloud, appeared the outline of another dhow, heading north-westerly towards the Gulf of Oman. Radnor gave a low exclamation. And as his eyes grew accustomed to the place in the sea where he saw the little vessel, he calmly attempted to decode any conspiracy of shade against shade that might have manufactured the effect.

Peeke appeared by his side. He was looking straight at the dhow, but he made no reference to it, only pulled out his pipe and rammed it between his teeth, the jets of flame illuminating misgivings behind his eyes. Shaking out the match, he inflated his chest, standing straighter, drawing in some kind of surety with the smoke, and becoming, for an instant, imperious, commanding, throwing his head back in a moment of agreeable self-assurance.

Radnor strained his eyes into the darkness. There was nothing there. He looked round at Murphy, at Peeke, then for a second or two closed his eyes, steadying himself against a sudden dizziness when he opened them again, continuing to search the empty sea.

Now he felt deeply indifferent, and frightened. He turned away, looking astern and thought of the little hut outside Port Sudan, and of Khadeja again, and in a moment when the ship lurched in an unfamiliar way felt as though he held the dense sphere in his palm, so concentrated and small, so wide, airy, diaphanous.

He believed he had, sometimes, made things happen. All right, he did not understand how or why, but it had always been real enough, and now as fatigue was finally getting the better of him, he couldn't care any more. He would flunk the test. Be found wanting. If it had to be . . .

But the darkness endured and the ship ploughed on. No sudden moves, no sounds, only the low hum of the turbine through the night, the soft swish of the bow wave, the muted figures and the faintest glimmers reflected in the moisture of the eye. No change. Then the form again, so shadowy, chimerical, caught in a glimpse away on the starboard hand. When he raised his glasses to take a look, it prompted Peeke to do the same.

'Anything?' Peeke asked, suddenly nervous, scouring the blackness. 'Nothing, is there?'

Radnor let his glasses fall on to his chest. 'Nothing. I'll be happier when we're clear of this little lot.' He jabbed a thumb towards the sky.

'You better keep me posted, Bob. I'm getting my head down for a while.' And, tapping the binnacle as he passed as if in confidential greeting towards Murphy, he disappeared down the stairway to his quarters directly under the bridge. Radnor followed him to the door, heard him descend the stairs, felt in the dark that the door had been securely closed and then returned to the front of the wheelhouse. He felt Murphy's eyes follow him; felt their readiness to dart back to the compass card, innocent, diligent.

He went outside. If ever he had felt *its* proximity, it was here, now. He could feel it. He could hardly articulate . . . such nonsense, but, now, all around, so close, in him, through him, and out there in the darkness, and, somehow . . . the breath of it! Radnor gave a shudder and in a fit to somehow rid himself of it, began to retch, bending low to throw up into the scuppers, to get it out of him. But nothing came. Whatever it was, why it was, he dare not think. He could not even describe the thing, only felt it, perhaps as some . . . inevitability.

Spinning round to go back inside, he noticed Murphy, his neck turned through ninety degrees, regarding him with distaste. He dithered, looked ahead, and again back towards Murphy still watching him, the wheel miraculously turning spoke by spoke in his hands, maintaining the course. Murphy did not waver and, if anything, scrutinised Radnor the more, the wheel still turning back and forth. He saw the quartermaster's features change, somehow separate from the rest of him, and in that faint soiled light thrown up from under his chin saw the white, clerical collar, unmistakable from his boyhood, the wire spectacles, the disapprobation, the disappointment. Radnor screwed his hands into each other. The Reverend Fry watched from behind the wheel, pinning Radnor to a place on the deck, until some subtle, indecipherable change took place, perhaps some particular combination of movements sent from the sea through the ship, releasing him, cutting him free of the deception, so that he saw the shifting eyes of Murphy again exploring the darkness, where he, Radnor, watched, concealed.

A sea change had brought about a slight alteration in the movement of the vessel, only slight, but enough to knock Murphy out of his sleepy regularity at the wheel, until a new pattern had established itself and he could settle again to thoughtless reflexes.

Something now impelled Radnor to approach Murphy, purposefully, like the shadow of a shark against the sand, until he stood before the quartermaster, the binnacle between them, his hands resting on the iron globes on either side of it, and Murphy, eyes on the compass card, feigning a stead-fast concentration.

Words; Radnor felt his gathering confusion in anything more than the simplest of dealings. He shifted his feet, felt the tightening of muscles about his neck and shoulders which he'd come to expect, almost like an incipient chorea, and writhed inwardly, forcing himself to remain still.

'What', asked Radnor after an age, 'do you find so funny about reducing speed?'

Murphy's movements were transformed by the question, there was vigour, more definition, more consciousness, making it seem as if it might be too tricky to steer and answer. The wheel flashed in his hands.

'Well?'

'What exactly would you be meaning, chief?'

'I think you know.'

Murphy, nicely secreted by his task, said nothing for a while, then, primly, 'There's nothing funny about reducing speed, chief.' And with a mixture of audacity and mockery, he lifted his head to look straight at Radnor, as though safe behind someone else's quotation. Provocative. He wasn't stupid. He knew there was something amiss with the mate. The old man had said as much.

The ship began to slide off course as the two of them considered each other across the top of the binnacle, the compass now rotating unseen, the bow swinging and the propeller thrusting the stern over, until the ship lay right across her proper course.

'Why's that?' Radnor asked with cynical patience.

'Why what?' Murphy said, his eyes still fixed on Radnor, standing up to him, but not so certain.

'Why is it not funny?'

'Time!' Murphy squawked, more unsure. 'Time's money, chief.'

This would not have been Murphy speaking and Murphy could see, as soon as he'd said it, that Radnor knew.

The strange motion as the ship wandered wide of her course brought Murphy quickly to his senses and he spun the wheel, the ship yawing and plunging as she came back on to her proper heading, an isolated trough producing a single, heavy corkscrewing motion, catching Radnor off balance and sending him diagonally across the wheelhouse; the rumbling of unsecured objects behind in the chart room, the report of a sliding door crashing to, the vessel shivering as she collided with a rogue wave, all adding to the mayhem and the feeling within Radnor that he, like a shadowy character in a dream, was melting away as the dreamer awoke.

'What's that?' Murphy sounded timid, but leapt at the opportunity.

'How should I know?' Radnor whispered, moving back towards the binnacle. 'What's your heading, Murphy?'

'Zero four six . . . zero four seven, sir.'

As Radnor started towards the chart room a penetrating high-pitched whistle cut across his musing and he swung back towards the voice pipe, removing its polished brass top before speaking into it. 'Yes sir.' He spoke flatly, and then put his ear to it.

'Everything all right up there, Bob?' Captain Peeke's disembodied voice, thin, anxious.

'Fine.'

'Felt like we collided with something.'

Radnor did not reply.

'Bob!'

'Everything's fine, sir.'

'Well, call me if . . .'

'Don't worry.'

Radnor put back the brass top, truncating the clatter of

Captain Peeke doing the same just a few feet below him and, looking up, saw the first tinge of dawn.

He continued his pacing as the light gradually informed the contours of the wheelhouse, everything coming forward out of the darkness until, in the first light of day, Radnor could make out the entire foredeck as well, and Murphy altogether visible now, undressed as it were by the light, nervous, foxy, treacherous.

It was now, on the main deck, with the night and, it was thought, the probability of the storm receding, that an occasional figure spilt out on to the hatch covers – pilgrims taking a stretch after the long night cooped up in the crew alleyways, their little shanty street dismantled; lifting their eyes towards the paler part of the sky, they stretched their arms in rapture and relief. Radnor watched from above, watched the little congregation as it grew, and the sea sweeping past, a flourish of brilliance. He seemed to lose balance for an instant, recognised as the ship rolled him nearer the smeared, leaping surface, recognised once more the pull, the witchery of it, and as he felt the dragging fatigue of his own struggle, shoved himself with all his strength towards the door of the bridge. Murphy watched from the wheel in the hardening light, saw Radnor stagger drunkenly towards him, lunging unsuccessfully at the binnacle as he was taken past by the roll of the ship, colliding hard against the opposite bulkhead.

Radnor recovered himself, and felt his head, having hit it again in the same place, the original injury attracting further injury.

The ship settled into a calmer patch of sea. Radnor leant against the bridge windows, sullen, watching the pilgrims prepare for prayer, devout, respectful, conscientious, scrupulously arranging themselves, ritually following the rule, the sea steely in the early light. Abruptly he turned to face Murphy, giddy, teetering backwards. 'What do you . . . do you believe, Murphy?'

When Murphy raised his eyes, he was not prepared. The grin which would have accompanied some waggish reply evaporated as it formed. The intensity of Radnor's appeal was instantly beyond doubt, and Murphy, though chastened, at last began, as he thought, to get the picture. He had been at sea long enough to have seen all kinds of people undergo that change which sometimes happens far from land. It might happen to anyone, though he couldn't imagine it ever happening to him, like the onset of a disease, the change sudden or gradual. The emptiness in people who'd been full and busy, as though some parasite fed on their thoughts. Empty. Once, he remembered, he'd seen a young first-class passenger run out on to the deck and vault cleanly over the newly painted rail, the sound of the paint unsticking from his fingers as he launched himself off the ship and into the sea. He had started off the voyage as a sunny, friendly young man, and in little more than a week had fallen silent and morose, staring for hours at the passing ocean.

Murphy knew that such things would never happen to him because he saw himself as too practical, though this immunity was supported more by his unerring cynicsm.

But now there was something about the mate's eyes that compelled him to regret his stunts of recent weeks. In that single tumultuous look, he picked up something of Radnor's terror, began to understand, like children persecuting another child, that they had gone too far. Evans had been right. Feeling in that extreme, his own insensibility turned in on himself.

'Believe?' It was hard for Murphy to look directly at Radnor, his eyes reflecting the luminous eastern sky. 'Believe? Well. A safe voyage, chief.' He grinned. 'And pay-off!' He took his hands off the wheel, rubbing them vigorously together at the prospect.

Radnor had placed his hands up behind his back and was holding firmly to the wooden sill below the windows. 'Pay-off,' he repeated.

Murphy, his feet set apart, hands wide on the wheel, didn't want to get into this stuff. Yet he felt in some peculiar way infected by the mate's turmoil, absorbed by it. He could only glance at him momentarily, when lifting his eyes from compass to bow and back. It made him uneasy. He didn't want to be asked about these things. 'That's right, chief, money in me pocket. Freedom to do what I fuckin' like!' He made himself grin, turned his head and winked, falsely unrepentant, defiant; and, as Radnor saw, uncompliant.

The pilgrims were ranged in orderly rows, angled across the deck. It didn't occur to Radnor, turning back towards them, that they might be directing themselves where they would not wish to, facing aft, slanting as they were across the ship, but towards the wrong side, the effects of Murphy's earlier sport, unseen now by its author.

Radnor rested his forehead against the glass and, not moving the position of his head which faced downward, allowed his eyes to prowl about the sea, the bow advancing remorselessly, sending out white frothy patterns across the water like outlandish lettering which quavered on the surface for longer than seemed natural, as though the sea herself betokened uncertainty.

The prayer meeting went on. Apart from the watches in the engine room and bridge, the crew slept and the great cargo of cement and pipes and cars and machinery waited in the dark below decks. Above, the light wavered, grew in strength, rising, falling, rising, steadily, disseminating the dirty skullcap of cloud, soon to be penetrated by that single blade of pure sunlight which briefly so lifted the spirits. When it came, glancing off the moist decks and steel plating, illuminating the ship, the superstructure blazing white, incandescent against the troubled sky, the imperious funnel still exhaling its vaporous breath and the masts flashing with the swagger of the vessel, when it came, this hard bright beam of sunlight locating and then accusing, Radnor was still in his place at the bridge windows, observing the prayers end and the spirits lift – the pilgrims, earlier so contracted by their fear, now like magic, so animated.

But as he shifted his weight from one leg to the other, about to return to the chart room for his sextant, as his gaze swept across the deck, something on the fo'c'sle head caught his eye. And in that half-turned position he froze, at first unbelieving, before his rational mind came to bear on what he thought he saw, ingeniously attempting to identify it, naming it, trying to explain it. But he could not. And still did not believe. He threw a glance at Murphy, now uncharacteristically pensive, his mind inward.

Although Radnor could still not believe what he thought he saw, with the hardening light he began to doubt, just a little, his unbelief. As soon as his watch was over, on his morning rounds, he would go forward.

Coming down from the boat deck, Radnor felt his legs weaken, and he steadied himself against the hatch cover stained with blood from the sailor's fall. He was appalled by the extent of the stain, but saw that it was already paler from scrubbing and the sun.

On the main deck, as each roll of the ship swung closer to the white sea hissing along the walls of the ship, he was again taken by the sense of some other life, indeterminate and beyond question. He walked as far from it as he could, threading his way through the waiting, expectant pilgrims, ever watchful, but in their narrow, scant circumstances, always

87

grave, courteous. Further forward, running his hand along the hatch covers, he felt the dry crusted salt under his open palm. Then the steady climb as the deck rose narrowing towards the steps – the steps, closer to the side again but lifting him higher, until he stood contemplating the windlass, the gypsy and the great metal claw which held the chain. Placing a hand flat on one of the links, the memory came of another fo'c'sle, another time, when a wire had parted and snaking back across the deck like a gigantic bull whip had severed a man's head, and this man, a seaman whom Radnor could not remember, had stood for a timeless moment, headless. But now the lift and fall of the vessel, more marked up here, enough for him to feel the recoil of his intestines, effected some movement right on the prow, dissolving Radnor's recollection.

The staff from which the company's house flag fluttered was waving drunkenly about; it appeared to be broken at the base, almost through, and hanging on by a few stalwart fibres. Radnor felt the first pulse of suspicion, his eyes darting about the fo'c'sle head, his hand still on the link but now so sure of what he would find that his legs began to move even before he had seen it. The bulwarks were painted a milky brown, and it had not been immediately clear that there was something else there of an identical shade, quite foreign to the ship.

Radnor was conscious of being viewed from the bridge and, checking his urge, compelling himself to remain still, he allowed the image of a splintered spar and shreds of sailcloth to sharpen, finally surrendering to it, and he squatted, settling down behind the windlass, unseen, the breeze fluttering the remnants of sail, now within that stillness, separate from all other, which follows violence. He looked again at the shreds of cloth laced to the spar, unmistakable, the hand-laid sisal, the roughly hewn wood, broken like a match.

After a little while, he rose quietly as if in a vacuum between separate lives. It did not now concern him whether Archie and the third mate or anybody else for that matter understood what he was about to do. They were too far away in any case.

Running his hands over the machinery in the manner of a desultory inspection, edging closer to the wreckage, he felt so surely that spirit which surrounded him, intimate, indivisible, and he acquiesced quietly to it. But as he was stooping to lift a corner of the ripped sail as if tenderly picking a wild flower, the spell was cut off by the shrill familiar note of the bridge telephone, inches from his ear . . . Out of inbred habit, he answered it.

A cluster of crackles, a crack. Archie must have struck the mouthpiece against something hard. His voice came through flat and stale, so that Radnor felt himself apprehended at the very point of deliverance – dragged back to a world made suddenly more loathsome by its familiarity.

'Is that a spar? Bob . . . is that a . . . some sort of a spar up there?'

Holding the telephone to his ear Radnor lifted one end of the heavy piece of timber with his foot to release the sail, and with his free hand began to push the remains of what he knew to be the dhow's rig over the side, so that eventually only the spar was left, anchoring everything to the ship as the mass of rope and canvas swung and flapped in a slow arc just above the sea and the constant turn of the bow wave.

'We seem to have collected some flotsam,' he heard himself say, remote. One good nudge with his foot would send the whole lot swimming away with the wake, but he held on.

Once there would have been no question; he'd have had the ship turned around, the search for survivors begun. But now it was not so clear to him. It was as if his professional knowledge had become suddenly weightless, entirely arbitrary.

'What's that? What's that you're shoving over the side, Bob?'

Radnor peered over the parapet. A great scar arched back from the bow. This moment . . . He shut his eyes. He was sinking. He could not see. He did not wish to see. Safer, like the fugitive, to hide – an infidel among the faithful.

'Bob, I'm sending the third mate.'

And yet, as separate from the ordered world of the ship as he himself had become, and as curiously light-headed as he began to feel, there was still, he imagined, his own skin stretched like string, upon which he saw himself suspended, Archie's words tethering him – enough that he could still feel the horror.

All this while his foot had been resting on the broken spar. He'd felt the faint oscillation through the sole of his shoe, from the long swing of the wreckage so tenuously connected to the ship.

Some pilgrims were milling around the break of the deck, standing close to the rail, their heads held up towards the horizon – the uncertain sky, aware of the crouching figure on the fo'c'sle, as an arm of heavy cloud stretching forward from astern eclipsed the sun.

The third mate came pushing boisterously through the knot of people, breaking into a run as he came in view of the bridge. He trotted up the fo'c'sle ladder, youthful and in the sight of the captain and others, he knew, wholesome. And in this conviction, behaved according to their expectations. It did nothing to help Radnor; rather his evident paying court to the bridge – his backward glancing, his patronising manner – caused Radnor to withdraw further, clinging to the spar and losing most outward awareness.

'You all right, chief? You look as though you've had a bit of a turn . . .'

Radnor wrapped his arms more tightly round the dhow's wreckage, letting his head drop forward on to it.

The third mate, seeing his chief officer curled up like a baby, felt himself deviate from what he knew might be expected of him. His composure, threatened by Radnor's visible anguish, began to fail. But from this circumstance and only from this, he was also able to recognise something he could not help responding to, and instinctively, spontaneously, he bent forward, touching Radnor tenderly on the sleeve. It drew a brief glance, but in that fleeting moment brought his own world so much into question that he, inside his starched white uniform, sprang back, fumbling for the bridge phone dangling from the end of its wire. Beginning to speak, he caught himself on the edge of something he didn't want to understand. He looked down at the reduced form of the mate. Already he seemed to be renouncing him.

Radnor could hear, but at such great distance he could not make out the words. He was aware but only half conscious, as if from a heavy blow to the head. Gradually he released his hold on the wreckage, allowing it to slip away until the sea caught it and it flipped, like the tail of a great fish, and was gone.

He was being carried aft on a square of canvas. The faces of those who bore him turned down towards him, disembodied, featureless ovals looped around in a wreath above him. And beyond, outside of them, another, hopping or craning to catch a glimpse. Who? As they passed under the bridge, more faces close together turned down towards him. Then the funnelling of alleyways within the ship. From this other perspective: the steel deckhead, the austere lighting, unpitying, high on the bulkheads, and the figure from before, beyond the bearers. His own cabin, the family portrait by the bunk where they laid him – his father, mother, he as a proud young officer. Finally, suddenly, the awful sickness, alone, something he could not get out of himself, the ceaseless retching, the violence of it, on and on, into sleep.

When he came to, it was dark. To start with he had the feeling he had been placed in a darkened cabin, but then he felt the violence of the movement and saw through his port the wild sky and the sharp angular features of a high sea. His body felt boneless, slopping back and forth. He had woken at the instant when the weather, having deteriorated slowly, takes a sudden turn for the worse, when what might have started in the manner of a friendly brawl turns serious and a blow is delivered of such unexpected ferocity that the ship reels away only to be overtaken by another, and another, no one on board left in any doubt now about the kind of struggle in which they were engaged, comprehension detonated by flying articles exploding into the air of their own accord, and again and again the incessant creaking, groaning of the ship, sometimes intensified, compacted, to a hard, jarring, staccato crack.

For a long time he lay, letting his body swill from side to side within the wooden lee boards of his bunk. There was something unfamiliar, amiss, about the movement of the ship. He felt it in the liquid of his body. It came when the *Delta* hung suspended at the extent of her roll, then instead of recovering, she lurched further over, balancing there undecided, at last coming back slowly and then faster on to her other bilge – a curious limping motion attended by the portentous complaining of the vessel's structure. Radnor lifted himself on to one elbow to listen and to feel the ship more truly, but like a boxer or a baby whose head is just too heavy, he fell back on to the pillow, thwarted but still sustained within the struggles of the vessel.

In time he may have slept or dropped away into torpor but he was drawn back again, conscious all at once of a shadow moving soundless across his cabin, a column of smoke perhaps, dark and leaning before a rush of air, soon clearing but so startling him that he again attempted, vainly, to pull himself up.

Later, staring upwards from his pillow, he began to recall much of what had happened that morning, but not all. Already his memory had started the process of selecting and abandoning. He could not for example remember the clarity of mind with which he had approached the wreckage at the side of the ship in those seconds before the bridge phone had intervened. But he did know that he had never before felt the 'Sea' so . . . within him, as though he had, in continuing in the manner of his old life, crudely, clumsily, fought against something he could never hope to dispossess and which would never dispossess him.

He had seen many die at sea, and in the camps of course, but most at sea, and the guilt he felt – the guilt in surviving them – itself never died. It was there, always, reflected in the sea's face, scrupulously, meticulously, revealed. But more, this all-seeing which he sensed within the sea herself, the knowing, had to do with them, the victims, the dead.

Towards dawn on the following day, Captain Peeke left the bridge for the first time in more than twenty hours, making his way immediately to his chief officer's cabin. He was exhausted, intimidated by his own shortcomings as a commander – missing Radnor, and regretting his own want of some deeper kind of . . . aptitude, fitness for the job. He climbed and slithered through the ship, losing breath, perspiring heavily, until he came to Radnor's door, where he held himself against the heaving and pushing of gravity for some while before he knocked peremptorily (unheard above the general racket in any case) and opened it. Pushing it wide, the stench of sickness on the heavy mouldering air convinced him to leave the door on its catch and he peered in, his eyes first becoming used to the darkness before an awareness of a certain lightening, a dim luminescence beyond the porthole, and around it the little curtain, tied back, swinging out stiffly, a tentative action as of a limb moving nervously towards the inevitable point of pain. He might have seen more clearly the nature of the ship's hesitant roll in this, as Radnor himself had done – was doing. But he only thanked God (whom he seemed to invoke more often these days) that it was at last getting lighter. He could make out the mound of his chief officer's body, then, drawing closer, he saw the moisture of Radnor's eyes darkly glistening.

'Bob . . . are you awake?' But then, a tremendous crash, an explosion, the ship lurching almost on to her beam ends, throwing Peeke across the cabin into the corner between the bulkhead and the desk where he braced himself against the ship's recovery, and his return journey. The *Delta* seemed disinclined to recover, and, disorientated though he was in that convulsive disturbance of forces, he owned for a second or two the conviction that she would keep on going, until the accelerating rush back the other way drew the old familiar disguises over the unthinkable.

'Are you awake, Bob?'

'I'm awake.' Radnor's voice, deeper than usual, came from far away.

'Do you mind the light?' Peeke, as if prodded and jostled by invisible hands, pranced back and forth across the cabin as he spoke. 'I'll just turn it on for a moment', deftly flicking the switch as he was frogmarched through the personal wreckage swilling in tidal surges across the deck: books (nautical books, no other kind), writing paper, the part-finished set of chess pieces, a torch, a wireless set in bits, articles of uniform clothing, a cap with its gold braided badge, all floating on a swell of sea water and vomit. Peeke, in a futile attempt to avoid it, added a high step to his dance, but his shoes were already filled, his long white socks bearing the stain higher than his ankles.

'God almighty! Where's all this water coming from? . . . God help us!'

Radnor stirred: little popping sounds as his voice broke through catarrh but no words, then as he turned to face the bulkhead, away from Peeke, he said with a certain nonchalance, his voice again deeper, broken, 'The scuttle . . . it's getting in there . . . she's wrung, I shouldn't wonder.'

Peeke scrambled, clawed across to the port and attempted to screw it down tighter, water all the time weeping down in little rivers towards the fetid broth, the desecration sloshing about below.

'There, that's better, I reckon.' He held himself steady against another violent lurch before getting back to Radnor. 'I'll get this mess cleared up. Feeling any better now?' He had heard that Radnor had refused food, so they had let him alone to rest. 'We've had to heave to. Just keeping her head into it.' This was conveyed as information, a bald statement, but was in effect, an appeal.

'All you can do.' The required approval came, but from a voice again unfamiliar, almost, Peeke thought, as though it wasn't Radnor's, and he found himself hanging over him to look closer. There was another lurch, a heavy booming sound, followed by a furious shuddering as though the ship were being picked up and shaken.

'Christ!' Peeke whispered at full force between clenched teeth, then stating but again wresting some kind of reassurance, 'I thought we'd come through the worst.' He did not take his eyes from the mound of blanket and the mist of hair which at long last began to move, the blanket pulling away as Radnor rolled back towards Peeke, revealing his shirt stiff with sick and an altogether expressionless gaze. There was nothing there. It was as if he had gone out of himself. Peeke's shock was, in that instant, articulated by nothing more than an expression of similar desolation, so that each now reflected the other.

'We have,' Radnor said. 'It'll get easier.'

The *Delta* gave another leap, falling into an enormous depression in the sea, rolling on to her side with a curious sighing sound, remaining there rocking quietly as if in a place of extraordinary tranquillity . . . until, surely, her bow began to lift, higher and higher, teetering for a moment as a great sea passed along her bilge pitching her forward at last, burying her nose in so deep she seemed to stand on end. 'God! . . . Could've fooled me!' Peeke said, still looking for more comfort, but now with evident relief and even a kind of bluster.

A time passed when nothing else was said, when Peeke, bracing himself against the throws of the ship, tried to use the emptiness at least to suggest, 'Well yes, here we are, both of us, together in this', but there was not even that sense, in this place where everything seemed to have changed irrevocably.

And so it was the disappointed, somewhat rebuffed and certainly solitary figure of the captain who finally inflicted the news, which Radnor already knew, that they had found no survivors. 'We saw wreckage,' he said at length, pulling his lips tightly round his teeth, and drawing air in with a hiss before delivering the blow; 'plenty, but no people . . . no people, I'm afraid.'

A little later, he started to ask Radnor about it, about his watch, exactly when he thought the collision might have occurred. But it was no use, no use. For all the reaction he was getting, it might have been a dummy lying there. In the end he found himself talking to fill a vacuum, but somehow the vacuum was never filled, and he'd slipped out discreetly, having finally acknowledged that Radnor was simply not with him any more, if indeed he was even awake.

Radnor was roused finally by intense light slashing across his closed eyes so that when he opened them it was with caution, shielding them with his raised forearm, as if to intercept a heavy blow. The day was well on, and now the sun, briefly showing through an early fault in the heavy, boulder-like cloud, defined the wild motion of the ship by slicing up into dazzling splinters the small space in which he at once felt himself to be imprisoned. But everything was in place, the little cabin neatly arranged, all was chocked against the movement, the deck dry and clean, the air sweet. He rested back on the pillow and saw that it too was fresh and that his old soiled shirt had been removed so that he lay there, his chin against the hill of his brown chest which rose and fell to an even rhythm in striking contrast to the surrounding but waning violence of the sea. Although he remembered the events of the last hours, recalling them in detail, he knew that at the time they'd happened, his awareness of them had been incomplete. He remembered for example the fo'c'sle head, the discovery of the wreckage, his acquiescence – the commitment so nearly made, being taken below on the canvas, the face in the crowd he couldn't place, Archie's visit, all these things . . . but it felt now, as clearly as he remembered them, that he had seen them from far inside himself, from where it seemed he could no longer operate his outward form – a kind of paralysis perhaps while remaining conscious, but this consciousness different, unfamiliar, where the immediate world though entirely identified, recognised, was of no account. But now he felt he was in some measure returning to his old self, the journey, though, having so sapped his strength that he felt he had been in bed for weeks.

Some time later a steward brought him soup and he levered himself up into a sitting position to drink, drawing his knees up and remaining with his back against the bulkhead, cradling the mug between his hands for a long time. But when at last he tried to take a sip, he found the mug to be empty, only the dregs remaining, and placing it between the fiddle rails on the little shelf next to his bunk, he could not recall having drunk it, until in due course he became aware of an evil fatty taste which he began to bring up into his throat, and he was sick again into the bucket which had been roped to his bunkside.

Later still, he may have slept, but opening his eyes at last on to the wave tops swinging past his porthole he saw the sun glancing off their high brilliant combs which now and then fell into themselves, a spent force, dropping with the wind. He dozed again, aware of someone coming in and going out, then slept soundly until evening when the ship's smooth wake once more threw its shimmering, streaming patterns on to the deckhead.

The next time he awoke he felt more wide awake than ever. In an instant he understood what must now lie before him. He could not remember when he'd last felt such simple lucidity . . . perhaps as a child? But it was really only that he had awoken resolved never again to risk leaving himself open, vulnerable in that certain way, to the sea – seductive in its images, informing as always his seafaring life, blessing and afflicting it with a survivor's guilt. It had undone his trade finally, he was now sure, but it would not, he had determined, consume him altogether, at least not yet; this he must have decided while he'd slept, knowing it the moment his eyes opened and knowing also exactly how he would go about defending himself. Indeed the purity he had begun to discover when he carved wood went beyond mere defence, drawing him in so that it became the sole reason for his struggles, the purpose of his labour transforming itself from escape to pursuit, and all within a kind of enduring innocence, despite everything.

As he contemplated the reflected wake lighting up his cabin, his gaze fell on the set of chess pieces now drying and at rest in their box and he remembered something of the release he'd felt in their production. He set the memory firmly in his mind so that he would never forget it, conceding what he believed he'd known since he was a child: that these fragments of wood offered a meeting place for his instincts, a haven or asylum against the immeasurable, and so he made a commitment then, lying in his bunk, gazing up at the strange designs flowing over his head, to a different kind of struggle, one which he'd found only in his carving, mumbling something repeatedly under his breath, like a mantra.

With this brightening, he shifted his weight on to his elbows ready to swing his legs out on to the deck, but abruptly checked himself when he felt the wet around him, the sheet saturated and with the sour smell of urine, childish confusion as yet still, somehow, unextinguished; bringing back the panic, so stark and pure in his memory, when at the age of six he'd started to wet the bed, away at school for the first time. The stench was now passing on the same disgrace and humiliation he'd felt then, and recollections of punishment to come. He eased himself up and out of the tunnel of bedding, feeling the vestiges of dizziness, faintly at first but then more insistent, and sat up precariously to look about him.

The world which was really so little his own, but which he had flimsily constructed inside his cabin, had been violated, everything now being tidy and in the wrong position. And seeing his few things put where they should not be seemed to make the place some other person's, until, that is, he found himself blinking at what looked like the spine of his missing blue sketchbook. The sight of it sent his eyes ranging all round the cabin, not knowing what exactly he was looking for, but searching anyway, scrutinising every place but where the book was, as if saving up for another first sight of it, and in time turning back to it to confirm (against the gathering unfamiliarity of all else) its reality. The flooding may have dislodged it from the hiding place where it had been all along. Radnor fought to get out of his bunk, struggling against the tangle of wet sheets, shakily standing at last holding tightly to the lee board. Dropping carefully to his knees he crawled the few feet to the desk and pulled himself up to a standing position, feeling he had little balance, gripping the edges of the desk, and with one hand lunged upwards towards the book, grabbing it before he toppled sideways, breaking his fall the best he could but pitching over and rolling eventually on to the deck, knocking his head, as he seemed to keep on doing, in the same place.

Unconscious for a second or two, lying with the book on his chest, he rolled limply with the ship. Very soon afterwards, as he came to, he saw his door closing discreetly, the handle carefully released from the other side. For a while he stayed in the same position, not moving, staring at the door, then, with one hand, he held up the notebook, turning it round before his eyes, cradling his bruise with the other, and threw it over his head to land on the pile of bedding in his berth, this, before rolling over and following it, first crawling on all fours, then pulling himself up to stand uncertainly alongside his bunk.

Feeling weak, out of breath, half sitting on the lee board watching the sweep of the sea through the scuttle, he felt the waves' energies spent, like a pack of wolves, falling back out of puff, their tongues splashing about, and the ship steaming on, outdistancing them. But he understood, dreaming across the waters as they arched past beyond his porthole, that as one event attracted another in that inviolable progression, the sea was only waiting, watching. It was irresistible now, this pre-sentience, and he turned back into the cabin to the little blue book with its shades of hope, its pages puckered by the wet.

In the days that followed, Radnor grew stronger though he spoke not a word. Not even to Archie Peeke, who visited several times. On these visits, Peeke invariably brought up the subject of an inquiry, that there would probably have to be one. But even that failed to ignite communication. Radnor, engrossed as he was in his work, of sculpting, sketching, scribbling, appeared almost unaware of Peeke's presence.

Once, to absolutely no effect, Peeke bellowed, 'For Christ's sake, Bob, what in hell's . . . eh?'

Besides taking an early dislike to him, Angus McIver had always had his suspicions about Radnor. He didn't know why exactly, nothing definite, just feelings. And no doubt now he felt these feelings to be so wholly vindicated he could not deny himself just one sneaking visit to the chief officer's cabin.

He found Radnor squatting on the deck surrounded by a mess of wood shavings and sketches. Pushing the door wider, he attempted a greeting, to which Radnor looked up without a word. Then he moved, uninvited, a little further into the cabin, keeping his distance as though skirting a dangerous animal.

Very soon, as chance would have it, Peeke appeared.

'Angus, you here?'

There was a momentary exchange of glances. From McIver a faint suggestion of an admission. From Peeke, confusion. But their attention was immediately drawn back to Radnor, who seemed impelled to ignore their presence by working faster, scribbling, crossing out, screwing up countless pieces of paper. McIver shook his head at Peeke, whose perplexity allowed only a flicker of disapproval. They both looked down at Radnor with an earnestness clothing their own particular anxiety – seeing him, not seeing him, and what it was he worked at so furiously. They watched, mesmerised, as if being charmed to stay and contemplate his skill.

Finally, closing the door soundlessly behind them, they crept out.

After they'd gone, Radnor continued to work at speed before his attention abruptly wavered. Putting down his pencil, as though hypnotised by a thought, and with whatever it was he'd been doing screwed up in his hand, he clambered to his feet as though he'd suddenly been alerted to something. There he stayed, bewitched by the sounds of the sea foaming past his open porthole. He dragged himself over to it, tossing the screwed-up paper out. Then, pushing his head through, he watched the white ball in the frothing wake float away like a gull with its tail cocked up. He watched it recede until it disappeared on the ironed-out path of the ship.

Ahead, the long knife of the bows went on dividing the sea in a tumble of breakers, as the air was filled with a warm salty mist and somewhere within it was the broken quadrant of a rainbow. Through it, Radnor began to sense the first suspicion of a great shoreline not far ahead.

For a while he remained there, searching forward, his head well beyond the limits of the ship. Whatever he did, it seemed he could never escape his feeling that, like a hail of falling stars, matters were being drawn in their fall towards each other, as well as to some altogether vaster body. But for now, in all the ship's dark side as it passed by in the ocean, carrying its community and cargo, all together, all one way, there were only his eyes to see the great hump of the whale's back rolling on and on, finally throwing its tail flukes high in the air, so that for a second it looked like a monstrous sea flower, dark and sparkling, before it withdrew to its own clandestine garden below.

Supporting himself by the rim of the scuttle, he went on looking out across the sea, its surface, as he saw, sometimes falling into a reflection of his own drawings: the countless silenced mouths, the men he had known and those he had not. And he, the survivor.

He understood his guilt, understood that in hearing the call and escaping from it he had broken a natural law of indivisibility. He had put himself on the outside, or perhaps he had been put on the outside, and now he had betrayed, or been made to betray, everyone. Every thing. On both sides. The offence was so far beyond question, his guilt so far beyond measure, he felt squeezed, suffocated, between two merging, unstoppable attractions.

Towards evening the ship passed over into shallower water. The vibration from the engines gone, she floated free, unfettered by direction for the first time in days. Craning his head through his porthole again, Radnor looked around for the pilot, but saw only the shallow sea stretching away green to the line of the coast, the scent of land ferrying out to them on the dying breeze.

He had known this coast, and faintly recalled the clarity and promise of a former time, but even then (he could not be sure) he might also have held some kind of foreknowledge.

★　　★　　★

Even now, at this stage, with his determination to go up on deck, there was a certain hope that these things were not so. He decided to go to the boat deck, working out the best route for handholds, staging posts in case of sudden loss of balance or strength. Rising and moving carefully towards the door, the very slight movement of the ship was still enough to unbalance him, the vague nausea and tightening in his lungs still haunting him. Standing, one hand against the door as a prop, the other gripping the handle, he could not allow himself that quickening of spirit he clearly felt. He tried the door. It didn't budge. It had been locked from the outside. Then, almost on a reflex, as though such a thing had been expected, he swung back to his desk to call Archie Peeke.

A rattle of apparatus as Peeke lifted the receiver and listened.

'Archie.'

'Bob . . . ?'

'It's my door. It's locked. I've been locked in.'

Silence.

'Archie?'

'Yes I'm here.'

'You know about this?'

'Bob, I'm just so pleased to hear your voice. The door, yes. We thought . . . we couldn't risk . . .' There was a sound like the inside of a sea shell as Peeke slid his hand across the mouthpiece. 'Look I'll get someone down there right away. You're sounding . . . better!'

Radnor replaced the receiver in its socket on the bulkhead. He was shaking, and wet with perspiration. With his back against the bulkhead in the corner of the cabin, he slid slowly to the deck, where he sat with his knees up, his head resting against the side of the desk. Closing his eyes he moulded himself into the shape of the corner. His cheeks stuck to the wood of the desk as he slid down its side and back into sleep, so that his features were pulled upwards on that side of his face like some morbidly delighted mask, while on the other they fell down in desolation.

In sleep he was aware of being shaken, but he could not yet escape the dream. It stretched away beside him: the flats and tributaries of the Ganges baked dry in the bright sunless heat, dry fish and creatures blown about on its surface, and blood from the primitive scaffold inching forward in channels, a meniscus of crimson over shrunken mud which trembled, not with the breeze, but with the pulses of a living, shuffling line of men made compliant by the persuasion of their own minds. And as he receded, disengaged from the line, those nearest the makeshift structure turned as they passed, and he knew them all. But the executioner, pious, dutiful, blood-spattered in his white cape, would not permit him to look away into the darkness until it was over. So he saw the knife flash and flash against the white sky and he was choked with a rage against himself.

Now the roars in his throat were heard as faint whimperings by those shaking him and he found himself being lifted tenderly by Evans and Murphy, whose presence, as he slowly surfaced, he could neither fathom nor properly assimilate. He prised himself free of them and stood with clenched fists. Archie Peeke stood before him, while the two quartermasters remained on either side of him looking expectantly towards their captain. Peeke waved them away, seeing them to the door, discreetly closing it behind them.

'I had to bring 'em,' he apologised, turning round. 'I didn't know what to expect. You might've . . . God knows . . .'

Radnor relaxed, unclenched his fists and with a deep breath cast his gaze out across a bloodshot sea.

Peeke went on, 'You've been very sick . . . and, well, I hope you're over the worst.'

Radnor, without moving or lifting his eyes, whispered, 'Might've what?'

'Might've . . . had another turn. You don't remember?'

But Radnor continued to gaze at the water, his face fiery in its reflection, then he turned to contemplate Peeke before he said, in a voice half spoken, half whispered, as though he had lost it somewhere in anger, 'I remember everything.'

Peeke's expression was pulled downwards by the little whirls of muscle on either side of his mouth, his visible consternation then fixed in the familiar way by jamming his pipe between his teeth, but this, though genuine in itself, appeared to mask relief and a rekindled hope at the possibility of some kind of dialogue. And, no sooner had the pipe gone in than it was yanked out again, Peeke's mouth working in anticipation of words long before they came.

'Remember everything? Surely not.' He shook his pipe at Radnor's bunk. 'You lay there like you'd been knocked senseless.'

'Ev . . . ery . . . de . . . tail.' Radnor felt again a sudden difficulty, an impediment to forming words, a fear in the understanding that he was being stopped, prevented from going on. But knowing there was one thing, just one thing Peeke must know, he did attempt to go on.

'Archie, I have to . . . don't think I . . .' but hardly had he begun than he felt his voice sink down into his throat, as if pulled there, until it made him choke, the veins on his neck standing out and he brought his hands up protectively.

Peeke moved to help. But Radnor shoved him away, slumping back on to his bunk, eventually wiping away the bubbly saliva from his mouth with the back of his hand. 'I don't know what happens . . .' he said.

Peeke stood back. His attentiveness now seemed to change to the kind of anger that a child might feel for a recently dead parent: rather an admission of his own needs than any real consideration.

Radnor recovered his breath and there was silence again between the two men.

Somewhere between the thought and the word was the dim world in which Radnor groped. He began to fidget, feeling a discomfort in his body, almost a stiffness, an unease which made him work his limbs as though gathering momentum to see him out of this.

Peeke had noticed the sketchbook lying on the bunk. The sweep of his gaze tripped by it.

'You've seen this before!' Radnor picked up the book with its crinkled pages and turned it round in front of him.

'Should I have done?'

Radnor put it down, sliding it under his pillow. 'Doesn't matter.' He began to fidget again, feeling the tightening in his throat before he'd even opened his mouth. 'I . . . need to say . . .' His face reddened. It felt as if he were being throttled, or being held underwater. And he clicked his fingers at some paper on the desk. Peeke dutifully brought it over.

Radnor began by quickly sketching the sea. He had become so adept, so rapid at it that he had almost finished before Peeke's confusion had turned to curiosity, and he, Radnor, was already writing underneath, though haltingly, then returning to the sketch, adding detail, something else emerging. Peeke, by this time absorbed by the sheer fluency of it, delighted by the spontaneity of it, had forgotten for the moment the purpose of it all, especially as he began to make out a fine impression of the *Golden Delta*, and for one vain moment he felt pride in his command. But the mood of the circumstance quickly returned as he began to read the words, his face expressionless. Then he re-read them, staring at the page. Soon the old familiar expression returned, with the pipe, which he lit in huge bursts of flame, a stuttering beacon. He sat down at the desk without a word and began appealing in low tones towards the bulkhead, his pipe bobbing with each emphasis.

'Is this supposed to be some kind of joke? Whatever makes you think . . .' He went on staring at the bulkhead, slowly shaking his head, the smoke beginning to make his eyes smart. 'She's all right. Of course she is.' He stopped, looked at Radnor. 'Are you seriously suggesting . . . Whatever is the matter with you?'

There was silence.

In due course Peeke said, 'Look, I've radioed ahead for a doctor. He'll be coming out with the pilot.'

Radnor's only reaction was to pass his gaze across Peeke's. Their eyes met for an instant only.

Just then a loud hammering began on deck and a whirring of blocks, the sounds conducted all through the ship. Drumming activity, cries, chatter beginning to drift in through the open porthole. Archie watched Radnor for some reaction, but none came. From the shore wafted the scent of a spicy breath still rising from an earlier heat, the cooling pungency of the day's business settling over the sea with the evening.

'Well . . . I'll best be topside now,' Peeke said in a ridiculous attempt at cheeriness. Then as if giving assurance, 'Won't be long before the pilot.' He circled towards the door, and in an even more futile attempt at normality said, 'Might, just might have to anchor outside I understand.' He hovered at the door, unsure how to round off his visit in the face of such destitution. 'I'll be . . .' and he diffidently indicated with a flick of his head that he was going, silently reversing, into the alleyway.

A while later from deep inside the ship came the ringing of the engine room telegraph. Radnor listened, restless. He

108

had slept again. The deck operations were over. Perhaps had been for some time. He could hear the clamour and excitement of the pilgrims lining the rail, impatient for home.

But before he resumed his expedition to the deck, he worked his way cautiously around his own accommodation, a warm-up for the real thing, gaining a little assurance as he went, and all the while, from outside, he could hear the excitement rising, a babble of cries, as the ship approached the shore, the pilgrims' voices evolving into heroic banter. A deeper, more confident note altogether.

Radnor too felt his way towards some kind of frontier as the depth of the sea decreased, the ship bouncing in the shoals, the keel only feet above the bottom as he, almost completing the circuit of his cabin, caught sight of himself in the mirror, creeping about like a trespasser.

Later, he thought the boat deck wider than he'd remembered, whiter, a hot blast of oily air from the funnel sucking across his face as he pushed open the accommodation door, resting briefly, propped up in the aperture, feeling confronted, dazed by the open air after so long below. Then, when he was ready, he stumbled the two or three paces to the rail. The ship was manoeuvring. And towards the shore, a mile or so away (the cranes and warehouses of the port now clearly seen) a launch at speed threw up a bow spray which on the still water appeared like a white butterfly on the surface. Radnor leant heavily on the rail, watching this insect grow, its movement and direction even and constant, until at some point it became the pilot boat, its tiny dark body the triangular section of the bows, making directly for the ship. As it approached, the wings of the butterfly drooped and hung as the boat settled deeper into the water. Two men at either end in faded blue overalls brandished boathooks, and in the centre, clustered around the cramped wheelhouse, stood two or three in whites, the ubiquitous uniform from the West, naval hybrids worn the world over. Behind them, standing quietly but uncomfortably, a shorter man, also in whites, though with no epaulettes or peaked cap, a fat Gladstone bag in his hand. Radnor fidgeted, watching, unmoved, the launch nudging alongside, the pilot stepping neatly on to the ladder, running up the side like a monkey. And then the doctor, his bag before him, sent up on a heaving line, his ascent wary, circumspect, often stopping to check his safety, looking up to the faces peering down at him, or below to the bottom of the ladder dipping into the slot of dark water between the two hulls, or at his hands and feet, assuring himself he was still properly connected to the rungs.

Once the pilot and doctor were safely aboard, Radnor stayed for a time, watching the launch speed homewards, the white wings lifting again. At some point he turned towards the bridge wing where Peeke was, and now Radnor saw that he had been watching him. Their eyes met and Peeke looked away towards the shore then turned back into the wheelhouse. Radnor understood that Archie had reached the end. At that very moment, he thought, Archie was probably in the act of abandoning him, pushing him away with the contempt he would feel for a puzzle he could not fathom.

Towards dawn the following morning, Radnor woke into deep slanting shadows thrown on to his deckhead by the lights from the dockside. For a second or two he forgot everything. Unconscious of his life, he gazed from the darkness as if for the first time. Until, finally, little by little, the ice of a featureless plain melted and he remembered the evening before.

There'd been no anchoring off and the pilgrims had disembarked as night fell. The process had been oddly silent.

The excitement had been there still, but now it was contained. Bracing their bodies, almost holding themselves in, they had filed down the gangway on to their home soil, orderly, solemn, certain, the natural energy of homecoming subdued by the nature of their journey. They had filtered between the warehouses in groups, secure, and away from the ship at last. He'd watched, recognising some of the faces as they'd looked back at the ship. They might never embark on the sea again, never feel its seductive petition, embracing it or evading it as they might, compelled to remember what they had chosen to forget.

And of course there'd been the doctor, knocking faintly on his door, and coming in holding out his hand, which Radnor had taken. Looking down he'd been astonished to find the doctor had had two thumbs on his right hand, a second one growing from the base of the first and wrapped tightly about Radnor's. The doctor had gone on to examine him, then declared at the end of it all that, aside from a touch of heat exhaustion perhaps, he was quite fit.

The delicious scent of the land, its vigour, potency, and that of a millionfold struggle for life, pungent, a nostalgia for some time never lived but intimate, all the things only coming in from the sea will bestow, were already fading with the familiarity of it. The ship was a blaze of lights as Radnor weakly pushed open the accommodation door. The dockside was deserted other than a solitary figure, a watchman, standing before the wide doorways of the warehouse adjacent to the berth where, presumably, the ship's cargo would await distribution, and where, sitting on his haunches, the watchman enjoyed a smoke in the airless night, occasionally pinching his nose and blowing snot on to the ground, a custodian of the empty waiting spaces and the wide expectant dockside shaded by the high sides of the ship. On deck there was a kind of satisfaction for Radnor in the vantage the boat deck permitted over the land and the low sleeping city, and he wondered, supported in the corner of the rail, about the eventual homecoming of the pilgrims, swallowed up, as they would be now, by the interior and their own profuse, intricate associations.

He moved, transferring more weight on to his hands, running them along the wide scrubbed top of the rail, luxuriously over its saltiness, stretching his arms out straight like a vicar before his congregation, seeing the watchman's eye drawn to the movement. The sticky air hung in heavy curtains, obscuring all sound, smoothing it into a low whisper, with sometimes a defiant, isolated, report – unrecognisable, ricocheting in the emptiness of the night. He brought his hands together, rubbing them clean, and with a glance at the sky, the pinpricks of brighter light penetrating through from that other place, sauntered to the seaward side of the deck. The dock was black, but lightly on the surface was an elaborately woven design, of silver and gold, irreducible, reflecting light from edge to edge, connecting all sides – ships with the land and ships with ships, their derricks up, paused, hanging, caught in their race for trade. But something else intruded now on his consciousness. So enrapt had he been in the puzzle of light and shape and shade, in the act of forgetting in the only way he had found, that it did not for a moment stir him – but it was insistent, passing into the low mumur of a voice, and all the time a faint clicking which became, as it pulled him back, the flip of cards. He found he was standing only a few feet from Peeke and McIver. They had set up a table and chairs under the awning behind the chart room and sat smoking and drinking, Peeke from his toothmug, McIver from a tumbler. Radnor looked up at them from his patch of shade, unseen. Moths circled the single bulb crudely arranged over their heads as they played in its sallow light, opposing each other across the table, their faces waxy in the heat, their heavy arms bared and darkly hairy, each holding a fan of cards. From time to time they pushed their chairs back on to two legs and swung them forward again to throw down a card – something of consolation in this. And the words murmured, parallel with the game, but somehow not of it, but the game, for all that, still a comfort.

How long they played up there in that melancholy heat he did not know, but it was dawn before he moved again, waking, not from a full sleep but, it seemed, out of the night shade, when men appeared from the shore, many men, carrying their food for the day carefully wrapped in thick leaves secured with raffia.

Not long before the ship sailed from Karachi, Radnor climbed to the bridge for the last time and stood looking forward over the main deck and the open hatchways to the fo'c'sle – the *Delta*'s bow soaring over the dockside, shadowing macerated, agitated figures on the quay feverishly unslinging the final loads coming ashore.

On the red painted steel deck heat rose in a vapour that seemed to melt the legs of the dark figures moving through it; the serang shuffled about, as he always did, in a pair of old leather shoes without laces, several sizes too big, gloomily directing half a dozen seamen hauling a gantry aboard. They had sat on this makeshift arrangement of rope and timber all day, slung just above the oily waterline, knocking their knees against the blistering hull, lethargically painting out the long scar made by the dhow. The chippy at number one hatch had already begun to secure the cover, hammering wedges home against the battens; as the cargo handlers in the remaining holds streamed out of the darkness. And the young apprentice was strolling about in his white uniform, for all the world accomplished in the business of the ship, occasionally leaning over one of the coamings to search the holds. In time he would come to know what he was looking for, at, but for the moment it was the conformation and symmetry of his life he was getting to know, as he watched those spidery men, spare, bare chested, clambering out of the hatches into the harsh light, their eyes meeting his before he, faintly self-reproachful at some inner denial, averted his eyes, the little company filing on and away from him, down the deck to the gangway.

Radnor watched from above, recognising abstractedly the pattern, oppressed suddenly by his own detachment and disinterestedness. He spun round to survey the inside of the wheelhouse – everything in its place, the deck and the grating behind the wheel scrubbed white, the wheel itself of wood and polished brass, amidships. He sauntered over to it, standing behind it, holding it, as if he was steering the ship. The polished brass of the bridge telegraph at 'finished with engines' (its handles like two admonishing fingers) reflected the afternoon sun on to his features, pallid now from so long spent below, and his own disquiet – the dread which would not leave him – was affirmed by the compass repeater above the helm, locked on to its dockside heading. Letting his hands fall from the wheel, he looked about at the contrivances of his trade and stepped off the grating. Then, touching the radar, the telephones, the docking tele-graph as he went, in valediction, he slipped behind into the chart room. Here the business of the cargo decks, the vibra-tions felt all the way through the vessel, softened then dissolved altogether. Here, all was forgotten but the world of navigation. And the place, not in use, had a feel of some-where consecrated, breeding a sense of veneration, like the darkened theatre in the morning, the echo of the previous night's performance still there in the silence. Someone, the second officer probably, had recently been there, preparing the charts for the next stage of the voyage. As he moved about, Radnor touched things lightly, almost lovingly, running his hand along the top of the chart table, smoothing the chart which showed the coasts of west Pakistan and India, caressing it with the flat of his hands, dreaming. Then, slowly, he dropped to his knees, stretching out a hand, probing the air, like someone blind, not seeing the set of drawers which he almost touched, but holding his hand in front of them until finally, succumbing to a pulse of resolve, he grasped a polished brass handle set in polished wood, and pulled.

A battered wooden box, square, and at some time polished, sat inside, its top almost level with the top of the drawer. In the centre of the lid was a plaque, the engraving obscured by verdigris. Radnor carefully lifted out the box, got to his feet and set it down on the chart table. He rubbed the brass plate but the wording remained unclear. He had been content to allow the letters to fill up and fade over the years, though he remembered what they spelt:

FOR ALL ROUND MERIT AND ACHIEVEMENT.

and underneath:

R.W. RADNOR 1918.

He lifted the lid. There was his sextant, just as he'd left it the last time. It had been a special prize. 'Nineteen eighteen,' he muttered, gazing at it. The headmaster's special prize. And he remembered the hall full of smiles, the crescendo of clapping as he'd risen to accept it.

With one hand covering the sextant, he remained deeply abstracted, reliving the moment of acquiescence when, trusting the applause, quelling his own instincts, he'd received the polished box with its gleaming instrument.

Still preserving the memory of so long ago, he did not notice Peeke's appearance in the doorway. It was not until he felt he had absorbed every last crevice of it, and not knowing what to think, that he quietly closed the lid and turned towards the door.

Even though he had every right to be where he was, of course, Radnor felt as though he had been caught red handed, in a place he should not be. It was with hesitancy, a vitiating self-doubt, that he turned back again to the sextant in its box and lifted it out, drawing it to him, clutching it as though it might finally be taken from him.

The two men faced each other, silent, until Peeke shuffled aside as if to invite Radnor past, who, staring wildly, seemed unable even to move, as though bracing himself – his expression urgent, an appeal. And through it all, still clutching the sextant, he was powerless to assuage the fervent sense that he was trespassing.

'So you've decided to leave us at last?' Peeke's tone was harsh, yet his expression was of pity and fear confused. He seemed distant too, or rather separate, insulated, as if he was merely watching what was before him on a screen, attending but uninvolved. He went on matter-of-factly, 'I've been in contact with head office and both they and I are happy to carry you home – if you want – since it is a straightforward round voyage, as you know. Your replacement should be with us in Colombo. On the other hand, if you prefer, we could get you back sooner.' Here there might have been a note of disdainful patronage. 'You can see we just can't go on . . . If there is to be an inquiry it will be in Colombo, but I rather think there won't be one.'

However much Radnor might have wished to say something, to redeem himself, how was that possible anyway? Faces of Arab seamen swam before him. He heard himself saying defensively, 'I'll stay with the ship.' He was trapped, knowing that to attempt to warn Archie again, to speak of his foreboding, his knowledge, would at best attract ridicule, but more likely be seen as a further subversion of the smooth operation of the vessel, culminating, as he well knew, in his own confinement. Not only that, but of far greater consequence to him personally was the further betrayal of the Sea. In any case, they were on a course he could not hope to change. What was going to happen had already begun. It had, for all intents and purposes, already happened. The Sea. The *Golden Delta* could not be protected. Radnor bowed his head, staring at the chart with dead eyes.

Peeke protected himself, Radnor knew, by surrounding himself with the armour of competent officers, the latest aids to navigation, an unvarying routine, the familiar, and of course the ship. He rarely went ashore, and then only when he had to. Radnor himself, for different reasons, had been drawn closer to the Sea, a voice growing nearer, not to be denied, so that in the end his understanding had converged with it in one climactic moment from which he had somehow returned. But Archie would never, could never, drop his guard like that. It was all too clear to him where such things led. He'd seen it all before. As he saw it now. And he'd convinced himself it was a form of weakness.

Peeke shuffled uneasily and moved into the greater space of the wheelhouse. Radnor followed, with his sextant now in its box as Peeke, his back to him, said with a sigh in an exaggerated routine kind of way, 'We'll be sailing on the tide', and he looked out across the dock through the side windows towards the open sea which shone like shoals of silver fishes against the sun, 'that's if . . .' and he moved forward against the front windows, peering down on to the deck '. . . those bloody little barboos pull their fingers out. Idle . . . ! Look at that . . . what does he . . . ?' He yanked the window across, '*Jildi, jildi*!', his voice trailing away in defeat as he clapped his hands.

There was a void, a moment into which the general racket from the deck flowed back into Radnor's consciousness.

Peeke slapped his hand against the sill. 'We'll go anyway,' he said. 'What they leave, they leave. There's priority in Bombay . . . priority in Cochin. No bloody waiting for weeks outside!' Then, in an attempt to lift his chief officer's spirits, 'We'll be in Colombo in no time. Your favourite port, Bob!'

'My last port,' Radnor whispered vacantly.

'Well we . . .' Peeke took a deep breath, exhaling with a sigh, '. . . won't be long now.' He returned his gaze to the deck for a second or two before strolling out on to the bridge wing and into the raw hammering heat of the land. He longed to be away from it.

Radnor did not follow, nor even watch. After a while, he turned and slipped away down the bridge stairs with his sextant.

As the *Golden Delta* plugged southwards, the coast of India just out of view, Radnor kept mostly to his cabin, venturing occasionally on to the boat deck, where he would hang over the rail, dreaming. Until once, the patterns he divined there seemed to him to be moving across the Sea's trembling iris, and he retreated inboard away from it, feeling the infinitesimal rise and fall, and between, the Sea, watching.

For the first hours of the passage south Radnor circled restively about his cabin, or visited the deck to ponder the glare of the wake, its pronouncement of blind steadfast intent. Returning to his quarters time and again, he threw himself on to his bunk, sleeping fitfully, and always flickering in and out of his consciousness was the dream, the same lines of men snaking across the dried-up plains of mud, shuffling forever forward.

As day followed day Radnor, now entirely shrunken into himself, moved only between his cabin and the boat deck. Sometimes, though, he was overtaken by a rage to draw or sculpt something. It would come over him, not immediately on waking when he would lie far away, but after a little while, jumping from his bunk in a ferment of industry, and sometimes without bothering to dress. He'd remain all day, his *futah* wrapped around him, or nothing at all, and often like this, he'd be too occupied to eat the food left him by an anxious and watchful steward.

There were complaints about him. The boat deck had become, in a way, his spider's web. Crew members who passed by found themselves tailed, overtaken, confronted by him, perhaps to confirm something in his mind, which, when it was done, would compel him to shrink away. For a while, as one might imagine, the people of the ship did not like to see their former chief officer half naked like this. There were ripples of disquiet on board, but it was soon clear Radnor meant no harm, and the crew slowly came to tolerate his strange practices even though they could not understand them. And so the mood relaxed. And the sea, so inscrutably silent, reverted in their minds to just another patch of calm.

In a little while, Radnor had made sketches of all the crew, and, always in the background, the sea and the sense of its coiled power. Sometimes someone would attempt unsuccessfully to engage him in conversation. However he might have seen these interruptions, he did not allow them to draw him away from his work, for though he used it to defend himself against almost every moment of his waking hours, it was true he also found within it an intoxicating struggle, releasing him in certain measure from the world around him.

The calm seemed to intensify. The ship hammered on to the south day after day, derricks raised in readiness for the next port of call, her decks level and brilliant, and there was a growing, common familiarity around the ship with this crazy man whittling his lumps of wood, or sitting cross-legged against a bulkhead, drawing. He kept on, pursuing something, relentlessly, never seeming to find it. Rarely would his heavy frown, an expression of determined yet perplexed purpose, leave him.

Sometimes when he was at work on deck, he would lift his eyes to the sea, to the wake, a ribbon of straight lace, unendingly, intricately devised and erased, then resume his work, slowly bowing his head again. In these moments he would sense again his love for those places far from land, with their own mood, distinct, unique, caught perhaps in a second of sunlight or shadow across the moon, amidst a special architecture of waves, where, as the ship passed over, he would hold his breath. At these times, when he slowly returned to his labour he would feel again the affliction that kept recurring: the ball in his palm, so dense, so small and tight, and so huge and subtle he could never hope to encompass it within his arms.

The *Golden Delta* spent nine days in Bombay, discharging the mountain of industrial hardware once hammered out in the north and now crawled over, fingered, prized, incongruously exposed to the Indian sky. Wharf sheds gradually filled up, packed to the eaves, cargo disgorged and stacked along the quay crowded to the very edge; there seemed no end to it, this conjuring trick, going on day after day — cranes dipping into the holds pulling out more and more from the magician's hat. And the vessel, partially relieved at last, began to rise higher, her mute underwater flanks breathing the air for the first time in weeks, but robed in thick glaucous weed – weed which attracted a fine coating of lime dust, giving her a white beard which, when it dried out, lifted clear of the hull, rippling along the ship's sides in the hot breeze, sometimes parting to reveal the skin – a rusting, flaking rampart.

Radnor remained bottled up in his cabin all the while. No one came near except the steward delivering meals. And he worked, worked incessantly.

Then, as the ship dipped once more to the open sea, she settled into that long easy stride made possible by the great calm. Radnor found to his surprise that he did not mind spending more time in the open, on the boat deck.

The crew's familiarity with him was by now showing itself in clear and specific ways. Archie Peeke for example, although avoiding direct contact, would stare down from the bridge watching his old chief officer for hours, his face crossed and drawn down by a deepening resentment but salvaged as he turned back to the wheelhouse by an expression of piety containing it. Angus McIver, on the other hand, certain, functional as his engines, would veer towards him hoping to catch his eye, to transmit his distaste, offence, at his continued presence aboard, but failing, would snort or tut over Radnor's shoulder, if not directly at him, then at his work. The Indian crew, if any should find themselves there, would pass, suspicious, watchful, puzzled, arcing around him. Only the quartermasters appeared to show kindness; a certain bashfulness, demurring as they approached to admire his work, whispers of approval when they saw it, reparations perhaps, but more likely a purging of guilt. And one day Radnor, sensing something familiar about one of them, recognising features as he momentarily lifted his eyes, squinted resolutely at Evans.

★　★　★

The *Golden Delta* arrived at Colombo in the late September of that year, one of many ships lying to buoys or at anchor. Here she began again the business of discharging her cargo, this time into lighters which bumped around her in the busy chop, like offspring eager for food.

FOUR

RADNOR SAT IN his hut, his home for almost half a century, his old hands fluttering over the carvings of his shipmates, restlessly picking up each in turn, clumsily returning them to the table with a mellow knock, not always the right way up so that sometimes the little heads rolled over on to a promontory of hair or an ear or cheek, coming to rest askew – the whole company scattered over the table top, disbanded, after the years of queuing, of waiting, in their orderly file. Sitting back in his old easy chair, he began, with a sculptor's instinct, to run his hands over the deep wrinkles of his own face and the raised areas of cancer from his years in the sun; this, before stroking his long beard, letting it pass through his hands, so that it split into two streams, his huge fingers delicately working, as if playing a magical instrument which further nourished his memories. Mindful again of the heads, his fingers once more hovered around them, tremulously touching them, causing them to wobble about and come to rest.

These memories, like those of a long slow descent into illness, returned to Radnor with exceptional clarity and implacable constancy. But looking out over the estuary to the curve of the far bank, the tide now at its height, the familiar account of the end of the *Golden Delta*, the one he'd written in his book, remained obstinately ill-matched with the rest of the story.

He rose suddenly, in a kind of panic and, selecting the head of Archie Peeke, leaving the others strewn across the table, he hobbled out on to the little veranda and his place on the steps.

Here, in the sunshine, he sat in his habitual position regarding his patch of sand where he'd turned his back on the rest of the world, scratching, improvising, vainly he knew, following an ingenuity and resourcefulness he'd never properly achieved or even understood.

In the distance under the cranes, a dark rectangle lying across the water was being shunted from its berth by tugs. The ship looked more like a giant box. Radnor watched, juggling the small wooden carving in his hand, weighing it like a projectile. Then he began to study it, this wooden impression of Archibald Peeke. The pipe had fallen out on to the step and broken, leaving the mouth open at the corner. A fine likeness of that precise instant when Archie himself would extract it. Yes, there would always be a revelation then, he thought, however small, an admission, which would have been hidden by Archie's composure, itself entirely contrived by the very act of smoking. But now his former captain was unarmed, staring up at him from his own hands, pipeless.

The block of cargo which was the ship floated out into the stream, turning end on, where it stopped as if balanced between one manoeuvre and the next, until, after a time, it began to grow smaller, leaving the land behind, slowly shrinking into the sea.

Radnor watched as he'd watched the *Golden Delta* leave all those years before, her befouled, encrusted sides climbing high out of the water, stale and rank, the bow wave swelling, coiling back from the stem in a sparkling grin. As he'd watched her, resting in its box on the dockside where he'd bent to set it down, was his sextant.

Now, gazing at the point of sea where the container ship had been, he could feel the consoling familiarity of the story he'd written, so long a false comfort, feel it begin to fill the abandoned hollow of those other events, so faint after so much time that most had faded from his memory altogether. There was only the walk which held constant in his mind now, down a night road to the beach to lie for hours before dawn in the high surf.

He settled himself, leaning back against the top step, stretching his arms sideways along the deck of the veranda, head thrown back, looking up at the sky with narrowed eyes, one hand clutching Archie's sculpted head, the other tightly clenched into a fist around the ball whose minuteness and density he was still unable to reconcile with its unlimited size.

As he'd stood on that dockside, there'd been a thin tissue of cobwebby cloud spreading from the east, bringing with it a draught which had darkened the sea's surface. Only cat's paws at first, but, he imagined, at sea later, they'd have noticed delicate mare's tails flicked about the sky with deepening corrugations on the faces of the water, crossed perhaps by a broad underswell from the north-east out of the Bay of Bengal. And there'd have been that exhausting humidity. The barometer would have been tumbling. They'd have needed no telling then, that all these things pointed to a deep disturbance somewhere to the north of them.

If he'd been there, he might have taken up a position chocked in a corner of the boat deck, to watch the development of the storm and the ship beginning her futile labour against the rising confusion all around, as lengthening swells from the north-east continued to cross the regular pattern of seas. The clouds, first like rolls of barbed wire, would have seemed to clinch together, tighter, giving the sky a taut, crimped appearance. Perhaps he'd have cast regular glances towards Archie, for clues of a change of heart, some sign at least of a response to the wind and sea which had gone on increasing. But Archie would not have slowed down, nor altered course, nor shown any sign whatsoever of their predicament. He was sure he knew this. He would have steamed on, despite all protestations, as though nothing could put the *Golden Delta* from her course.

Still on the steps, his chin jutting upward and his great beard stirring like pages in the wind, his arms outstretched as if crucified, there was something hideous in the spectacle (if there had been anyone there to see), cadaverous, as if he'd absorbed the savagery and brutality he'd witnessed and it shaped him now, literally.

In that old head, flung far back on the steps, as if broken-necked, a typhoon familiar in its episodes began to blow. And he recalled, as he had done so often, his own hollow words, as he travelled on across his tale, his intimate companion for so long:

I saw the light, almost gone out of the sky as if an execu-tioner's bag were being drawn over the eyes of the ship, only lightning flashes illuminating an uncertain, shadowy place, where sea and sky merged without limits; and the high flanks of the *Delta,* leaning precariously away from the wind, showing as the only truly remembered shapes. Just the same, I saw myself, the only person above decks clinging hard to the ship, riding her, a clay particle of humanity.

In those flashes, the air seemed opaque, laden with water, and so it was difficult at first to distinguish what it was away to windward, insistently drawing my attention, holding it fastened through the darkness. I was staring blindly, but at what? It was not identifiable. There was no word. Though I went on attempting to translate what was probably some simple conspiracy of light, it would not come. Only the inevitable seemed to draw on as the pressure all around increased, so much that I thought the actual structure of the ship might suddenly buckle. It had crossed my mind that it was another vessel, moving in our direction. It was moving towards us, but it seemed too big for a ship. As it approached I could see that it could not possibly be, for if it was a ship, it would have to be driven sideways on to us, and at such velocity as to roll before it a high frothing embankment.

My experience now told me that this thing could be no other than a line squall – but as it looked, a ferocious one. But then, on deeper inspection (for I could not lift my gaze from it, my eyes puckering at the corners and stinging with driving rain and salt spray) I did not believe what I thought I saw. There was something confounding, mystifying about its movement forwards, and in the sacred designs fleetingly picked out across the watery air, which detained me. The real violence of the squall, concealed behind flowing white shapes, blazing high up against its dark face, eventually came home to me with an intestinal shock, throwing me physically to the rail. This dread awareness being that it was not beaten air behind the front where the swirling streaking patterns challenged my failing reason, but water! A wall of it, of sea, moving across sea, sucking the poor *Golden Delta* in as it came.

And now, for a second or two the ship seemed to sail into a calm, lifting slightly and lifting again, as if in a lock where no one had the command of her, and she floated, turning to face the inflowing rush of the ocean. Looking to the bridge, along the full length of the ship in a dazzling flash of lightning, seeing no one, I started towards the accommodation door, hesitated and understood I could never cross the deck in time. And in that same flash I saw the sea as I had never seen it, at such a height before the indifferent bows, a sliding perpendicular mass at whose summit quavered and tottered its pewter ruff, as if paladins behind water turrets sawed the air with their metal spears. And the ship hammering on, in the end undaunted, steaming, as it were, into the side of a cathedral.

I doubted if the vessel could survive the tonnage of water which would be released on to her decks. I did not stand, but crouched by the rail gripping it fiercely, looking back over my shoulder towards the bows, bracing myself for it, unable to judge the distance still to go, the ship now appearing to stop before a stationary wall, until, like a bomb, the draught of the explosion flew back to me above the tumult, and I watched the bows plunge into the edifice – the sea yielding to the shape, opening like a monstrous insect-eating plant, before collapsing. Not boiling and frothing on, the way it usually does when a big sea climbs aboard, but swirling deep, undisturbed by hatches, winches, deckhouses, uniting with the sea beyond the ship, with that strange momentary calm in the midst of it all; so that if Captain Peeke were looking forward from the bridge, only the masts would have shown, to announce he held his command still.

I felt the ship sink, then steady under her burden, the main deck now well below sea level. It was the kind of moment, after such a cataclysm, when arms are still held over heads, eyes tightly closed against the worst, but when tense expectancy relaxes towards caution – those still living begin to stir. I got to my feet on the curiously muffled deck, gaining confidence but feeling that the ship did not rise, pressed down as she still was below the sea, as though an invisible hand was holding her there until she drowned. For a moment I felt the engines, striving blindly, battling to release the ship from a fatal lethargy. At last I felt her movement through the sea, but then, as if she had reached that cataract at the edge of the world, her stem dropped with such violence that it uprooted me where I stood, sending me tobogganing to the other end of the boat deck, dashing me hard against the funnel casing where, partially winded, I fought against unfamiliar forces to struggle once more to my feet, but found myself held there, pinioned, made to concentrate on the ruinous vibrations of the engines racing as the propeller flailed to no purpose in the air. Looking aft, I found myself gaping upwards, along the impossible incline of the deck to the sky, the sea, as the ridge of the tidal wave passed along the keel; the ship's forefoot colliding then with the trough as though it were the rock bottom of the ocean itself, sending the impact jarring through her full length, and the sudden bite of the propeller again as it was slung back into the sea when the bows eventually lifted. Slowly, heavily, she righted beneath a thousand tons of water which began, in a lazy current at first and then in a boiling torrent, to fall aft towards the break of the deck. I could feel it under my feet, this mass rolling down the hill towards the superstructure, gaining force from a trot to a gallop to a charge as the gradient increased, until it launched itself on the ship in a bitter, white fury, erupting in convulsions, hurling itself about, a madness of destruction, smashing, tearing, wrenching, in every way, with such dreadful malignant rage and purpose without end, that the ship was brought up by it, shivering to a standstill, swept as she was repeatedly from end to end, so that though she still floated, she seemed merely to wait.

I had no time to guess at what kind of devastation there must be below decks, but found myself fighting for air, time and again spitting out salt water, hanging on to an eye bolt as I felt myself pulled through a torrent, first one way then another. I was aware that there cannot have been much above decks that had not been carried away. The lifeboats had all gone, the davits and falls were twisted and flailing about, much of the rail that I could see gone too or worked into a plait, the housing between numbers four and five hatches taken clean away as if with a single swipe from some mighty cleaver – donkey engines, bitts – I could not tell.

In another flash I saw the hopelessness of our position: my knuckles bleeding around the ring bolt, the blood welling up to be washed clean again, the sea strangely hopping around the ship in high pointed peaks as if an army had broken ranks and they were now no longer one body but separated into single units, fickle, unpredictable, pushing up against each other to catch a glimpse of the lynching.

The boat deck tipped wildly to port. I was swung round and saw my raw fingers tighten about the ring bolt. The ship did not recover this time, but listed so that the deck beneath me became a steep beach swept incessantly by a rising tide. There was only the smoke, spilling heavily like some preternatural alchemy, blown down the sides of the funnel, pitched as it was at such a crazy angle, suggesting still some living warmth within the darkened body of the vessel.

When the time came, the water shocked me with its warmth, and to be finally in it, a part of it, had the effect of purging me of my fear. I saw the *Golden Delta* listing so heavily it felt as I was swung upwards outside of her as if I were flying over her decks. The black mouth of her funnel was like the burnt beaker of some botched experiment. I saw the ship as she was, merely a carcass, the decaying remains of a misplaced cause.

From where I now swam, I could see not one human movement aboard. The storm shutters were up at the bridge windows, the dark hulk turned in on itself in a rite of self-inquisition. Then, indistinctly, I thought I saw the heads of two or three people in the sea closer to the ship, but the scene was so benighted even though it was the middle of the day and the waves and troughs too steep and chaotic, that it was impossible, even if they had been there, to fix their position, and I lost them immediately.

I realised I was being carried further off, perhaps being taken by a surface current, powerless against the continual tumbling over and over in the crashing seas, my breath repeatedly knocked out of me.

It might all have ended quickly, except that in the midst of that cauldron, two forms attracted one another. My body collided with something solid, and like a drowning spider to a leaf, I remained fastened to it. At first I couldn't guess what it was, only clung on unseeing, as it pulled me time and again to the surface. Eventually I managed to clamber on to it face down, gripping the wooden slats that seemed to me made for the purpose. Then it came to me, through the astonishing proficiency with which it rode the waves, that it was (of all things) a life raft. A simple square construction filled with buoyancy enough to lift ten men a few inches above calm water, allowing me, even in these circumstances, to briefly glimpse that I was at the centre of a little universe of debris, with the lifeboats, all capsized, nearby. There were crates, dunnage, lengths of taffrail, shapes that appeared to me familiar but for which I could find no name, and beyond, the ship settling, listing even more heavily, down further by the bows, great waves mounting and smothering her, breaking along the full length of the deck, her sidelights still glowing, insolent, like vanquished standards in the soaking semi-darkness. But all the while she seemed to be receding. I strained, through the seas, to keep my eyes on her. But then as if by sleight of hand, some play of light, at a time when I may not have been watching, the *Delta* had fallen abruptly, steeply, to port, and through the gloom against the paler background of her decks I wondered if I saw figures, dark comma shapes bent one against the other, moving almost imperceptibly about. Though I watched intently, great chunks of time seemed to be lost to me. I imagined I saw others in the sea not far off. Then, as the ship's stern lifted high out of the smoky sea, one tiny figure appeared at the side door of the bridge. The beam of his steady, inscrutable gaze homed directly, surely on me. The stern reached that point where it could rise no further, and a certain hollow was passed over between one instant and the next, between the lift of the stern and her going down, and as if at a nod, the vessel began her fatal slide down into the sea's throat, blasts from the release of air rising above the turmoil, until the stern itself, by now standing perpendicular, passed the level of my eyes. The sea boiled from the discharge of so much air. It seemed to hold back the waves, so that they merely crumbled innocently on to the place of her foundering, producing there for a time afterwards a disc, a pale altar on the flattened surface where she had once been, which grew darker by the moment, changing as the last breath must have been squeezed from the sinking ship, until – there was nothing more to show; the waves simply knitted

together over the spot, bequeathing the intensified emptiness only intimacies can arouse . . .

Before much time had passed, clinging hard to my raft,
finding myself flung to a peak maybe thirty or forty feet
up, slithering again to the trough, down steep hissing hill-
sides, the pressure and wind painful in my ears, I began
to paddle, frantically, vainly, nowhere. I bellowed at the
top of my voice but the force of the storm drove the
sound deeper into my throat. When the raft flipped at the
crest of a wave I was permitted something of a perspective on things. I looked about, but as sea followed sea, I
lost all notion of direction and I realised there was no
one. Even the lifeboats and debris had vanished and there
was only the hilly sea below a fallen sky.

A stage followed, a vacuum, where I seemed to have
no memory, of anything, other than the incessant lift and
fall of the raft and the moulding of my body to it. No
thoughts. I flattened myself against it, clutching it as if I
were growing into it . . .

Through the dark hours and dim dawns of the
succeeding days, the realisation came at last, that the sea
and the wind were moderating . . . And later, much later,
I felt how the light of the sun in the clouds was unshack-
ling me from my position, so that I could move again,
and I turned over to lie on my back facing the clearing
sky, tormented by my thirst and my wretchedness.

The old man remained spreadeagled on the steps, as he might
have been on the raft itself, pulling out the slender cord of
the story he had written, retracing his miraculous drift across
only a few miles of ocean; the particulars dissolving before
the one principal contingency, which must have been a fierce
south-easterly flowing current which would have carried the
little raft out of the Bay of Bengal to dump it felicitously

on the waiting beach, to what he publicly insisted (the words fortified against doubt by the printing of them) was his redemption, yet again.

FIVE

JUNE MORROW PUT her carrier bag down on the upturned skiff and looked about her. What a junk heap. It seemed that everything that floated past must wind up here: tyres, crates, driftwood, plastic bottles, fenders, net floats – what must he do with it all?

Mr Radnor was lying on his steps. He looked to be frozen in pain, or worse. She approached cautiously. In her hand she held two letters.

'Mr Radnor? Mr Radnor,' she whispered, close to him now, bending low. But there was no hint of awareness.

She picked up the sculpted head lying next to him, turning it around. There was something about it, a force, something. She didn't know. But she didn't like it and put it down again on the step.

Straightening herself, she was unsure now how to proceed.

But suddenly, he was squinting up at her, through one dark watery eye.

'Mr Radnor! Thank goodness. You seemed . . .'

'Not yet,' he said, choking as he spoke, his legs flailing about, as if he were sliding out of control, and sinking back again, abandoning his limbs, as it were, where he'd left them, but his eye still searching constantly, moving from June

Morrow's face to her hands, in which she clutched the two letters.

From the branches over them came whispers, rumours, conceding a moment of shared instinct.

He began to twist about and fidget, then came a rattling in his throat, a hoarse high-pitched wheezy sound as he attempted to form words, perhaps to say that after all this time he now wished to adjust kindly to her presence. He relaxed again, as his eye caught sight of her carrier bag. She followed his glance and with her face turned away from him, felt a spasm of tender guilt towards him.

'You had a couple of letters this morning,' she said, turning back towards him: 'unusual.'

She'd already studied the envelopes, of course. One was stamped 'The Wilkes Partnership', the other was rather official looking. She handed them to him. 'So I thought I'd deliver them myself and bring a few bits and pieces down while I was at it. If that's all right with you. Just a few of your usual groceries. Might save you the journey.'

He looked at her blankly, and held the letters close to his face, then at arm's length. 'My −' he flicked a finger at his cheek − 'magnifier. It's inside.'

June Morrow moved to help him to his feet, but he waved her away and pulled himself up on the balustrade. Now facing away from her and without a backward glance, he stiffly climbed the remaining steps, crossed the veranda and disappeared into the shack.

After a little while, June Morrow went back to the skiff, where she sat down to wait. She took a deep, quick breath and exhaled with a sigh. She held the carrier bag lightly between her legs, resting it on the sand, lifting it an inch, dunking it back on to the sand, contemplating the water along the shoreline and out into the stream, and the opposite bank rising towards stubble land blazing white in the sunshine. Further down the reach, a coaster was beginning its journey to the sea, passing between the moorings and setting little boats bobbing.

There was no sign of life from inside the shack. She would give it a little longer before taking a look.

She'd felt for some time, before any visit of any land agent – she'd felt . . . it was hard to say, but a kind of current running towards this strange and solitary old man. He must have almost come into her mind a great deal recently, but never quite enough for her to acknowledge it. It was like knowing something, yet not knowing one knows it, till later.

Before she had consciously decided to, she had re-crossed the patch of sand and now found herself at the bottom of the steps looking up at the open doorway. Quietly she climbed on to the veranda, crossed it and peered into the gloom.

Here he was, standing in the centre of the room, stooped, peering through a large magnifying glass which he moved painstakingly, word by word, back and forth across a large sheet of typed paper. She watched in silence, seeing the corner of the letter twitching in his unsteady grasp. When he'd finished reading, he pulled out the other letter, opened it with a finger and let the envelope drop to the floor. Again he read, and now when he'd finished, he stood staring up into the rafters. Then he said without looking round, 'All right, come on in, if you really must.'

Now he watched her. She entered, glancing all around at the world of carvings, her eyes rummaging into every corner of the place, the desolation seeping into her, and the carvings glinting in the darkness, almost heard from some other place, the only witnesses of his life. She looked over to the recently vacated shelves. The desolation of it.

When she had taken everything in, when she was finally sated after a long slow circuit, she turned to him and whispered, 'Did you do all this? There's so much!'

'All of it,' he said. He was thinking: if not her, then who? As he thought this, as he saw the flickering reflection of high water cross her face, he felt his courage begin to wane.

He said, choking again, his voice exploding through membranes of catarrh, 'There were more,' waving one arm in the direction of the empty shelves.

From where she stood she could see clearly the patterns in the dust, the discs of clean surface where they had once perched.

He pointed his thumb towards the table. 'Like these,' he murmured.

She went over to them, put out a hand to touch, hesitated for his approval, and picked up a small, highly polished one, replacing it almost immediately and picking up another which she did not seem to see as she surveyed the whole table.

'It's my life . . . in wood,' he said.

Whether she was thinking of this, or something else, she went on gazing distantly at them.

After quite some time she said, 'Is everything all right, Mr Radnor? I mean is there anything you want me to do?'

To begin with he made no reply, but he began to breathe more rapidly, as if taking shorter and shorter strides before jumping an obstacle.

'I . . . would you . . .' He seemed irritated with himself, then pointed to a chair for her to sit down. He remained standing in an oval of sunlight, contemplating her, frowning heavily. Then he too sat down in the chair opposite.

His deeply searching eyes seemed to paralyse her, but she was not disconcerted by this, but as she watched him contemplate her with such a penetrating eye and not knowing what he was thinking or going to say, she had the instinct that she would in no way be surprised by it. But she herself did not know what to say, or if she did, how to say it. Though she kept wanting somehow, to comfort him, desperately, to comfort him. She thought she understood him.

He shook his head, about to speak, opened his mouth but he too did not seem to be able to form words. He looked far beyond her and back to her. Until eventually he said, 'They've found . . .' though he did not finish.

She delved into the groceries bag to pull out the newspaper she'd kept specially. 'I think it's here,' she said. 'The *Golden Delta*? There's a photograph.' She fumbled with the paper, finding the place, taking it to him.

She stood over him as he read with his magnifying glass, watching him. She did not know what she thought. And despite the heavy pungencies of his old body, his filthy clothes, the sharp acrid whiff of stale urine, she was moved to touch him, to put out her hand and brush the saffrony skin of his cheek and his soft white beard.

He did not seem bothered or surprised by this, merely brushed her hand away as though it were a fly, as he concentrated on what he read.

The old man gave a grunt, dropping the article, the magnifying glass, his hands, on to his lap with a smack of crinkling newsprint.

'Things are coming in from all angles.' He was staring at the floor.

'Sorry?'

He looked up at her. 'I am the only survivor,' his words gravelly but unbroken. 'Survivor,' he repeated.

She moved round to face him, squatting in front of him. 'And . . . ?' she said.

But it seemed he could go no further. He'd become distant again, gazing over her shoulder into the shadows. Time sagged as she felt herself absorbed into his mood. A breath from the estuary, the tide on the turn, ruffling the newspaper on his lap. She pushed herself up and, as she did so, almost at the same moment he raised a hand as if to touch her, but too late.

'I'll just pop these things over here,' she said, picking up the bag of groceries and swinging it up on to the surface. Here, a blackened kettle stood under a smeared window covered in spiders' webs – except for a circular area in the middle, she could not see through it. Unpacking the things, she thought: it is too painful for him, but this is only the first time. He's not used to people. I can see he wants to talk. But how can he? I'll come back again tomorrow.

'There,' she said, turning back into the room, 'just a few things. Would you like me to make you a cup of tea? Or do anything else while I'm here? And then I think I must be on my way.'

He shook his head slowly.

She came over and placed a hand on his shoulder.

The warmth and strangeness of her touch no doubt induced a kind of loosening.

'Ha! One wants me out. And one wants to speak to me.' The exclamation, cracked out like a rifle shot, made her jump and withdraw her hand.

'Who wants you out? And who wants to speak to you?' she asked, indignant.

He shrugged, shaking his head as though nothing mattered and nothing could be done.

But did it really matter how he'd bought his time? Would they think it mattered if he hadn't told the truth? Did he think it mattered?

'Look,' she said, 'I'm going to go now, but I'll come back tomorrow, in the morning probably. I think there's a lot you need to tell me.'

But he needed her now. Not tomorrow. He knew it would not wait until tomorrow.

He allowed her to take the newspaper from him, and the

letters. He didn't care. She folded them neatly, smiling at him. He watched her turn to go with unfocused eyes, watched her hesitate and turn away again.

She knew she'd be back in the morning. Things had barely begun. She hesitated, turning back to him, as if to complete her goodbye in a way which meant it was not for long. But it was as if he didn't see her, as though there was something else there now, where she had been.

The slight movement through the floor as she stepped off the raft of the shack and on to the beach seemed to bring him back, and he struggled to push himself up and out of his chair.

By the time he'd reached the open door, she was well along the sand. Something seemed to be pulling him after her. Now he almost fell down the steps in his need to catch her. But the slope of the beach seemed far greater than it had ever been, and though he made some little progress forward, he staggered as though being tipped towards the tide, as though it swept a steeply listing deck, until he found himself standing in the water unable to climb back up this steep and steeper gradient.

He saw her still, turning up the deeply rutted farm track through the tangled woodland.

Repeatedly he filled his lungs but could not make a sound, puffing feebly, fighting against unseen fingers tightening around his throat, and he gagged and choked so pitilessly it brought him to his knees, helpless as he'd become to counter what it was he'd always known.

And he was surrounded by a deepening silence, where words for once had no meaning. And it did not matter.